Beyond The Wall

CONTENTS

Chapter I   Hawaii News 5

Chapter II   The Trip To Harpswell 14

Chapter III   The House 22

Chapter IV   Interesting Findings 26

Chapter V   Beyond The Wall 31

Chapter VI   Clover Lake 38

Chapter VII   Men In The Coffee Shop 43

Chapter VIII   Unknown Followers 51

Chapter IX   The Funeral 67

Chapter X   Chocolate Surprise 76

Chapter XI   Break-In 88

Chapter XII   The Portrait 100

Chapter XIII   For Your Protection 127

Chapter XIV   Flying Books and Hide N' Seek 133

Chapter XV   Taken 156

Chapter XVI   The Truth 168

Chapter XVII   Drugs, Thorns, And A Bad Attitude..... 186

Chapter XVIII   Bad News, Headaches, and Another Plan...205

Chapter XIX   Safe and Sound, Oh Is That Jello........... 222

Chapter XX   Released, Ah Home Sweet Home......... 239

Chapter XXI   Dark Tunnels and A Concerning Noise.. 250

Chapter XXII   The Last Clue 266

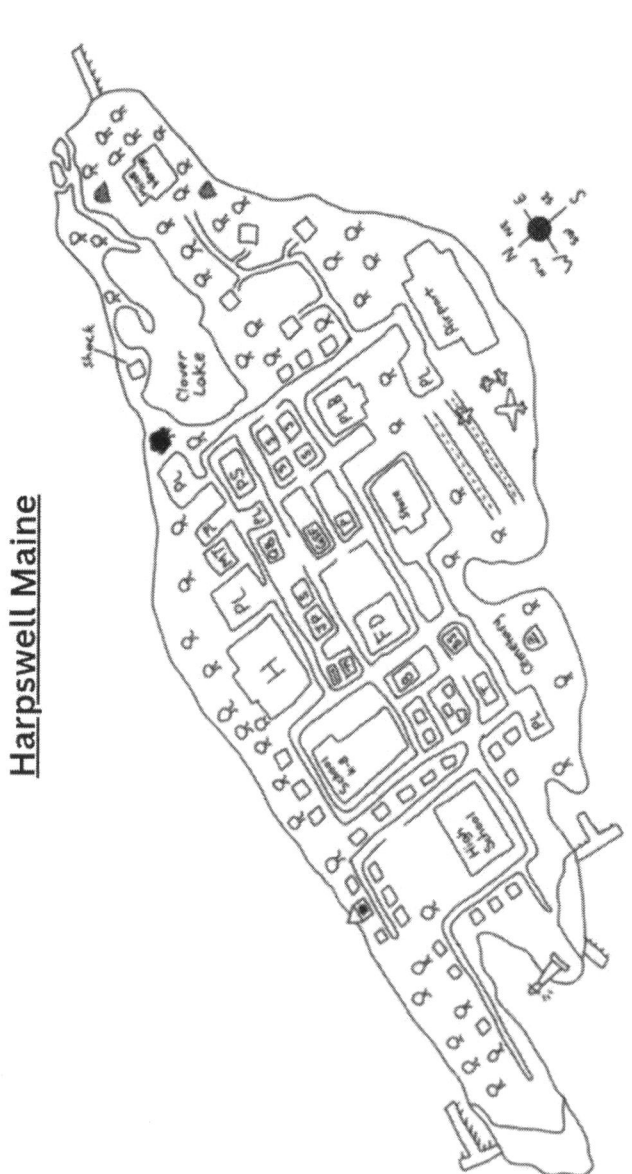

Chapter I
Hawaii News

The room was bleak, quiet, and incredibly dark.

Lily didn't know where to look first. Every object was faded, and she couldn't tell what she was looking at. Lily pulled her yellow bunny towards her body and slouched down in the bed. She then saw her door open, as the bright light from the hallway started spilling in. A tall man, as tall as her father, stood in the doorway holding a gun. Lily couldn't see what he looked like but could tell he was wearing a leather jacket. Terrified, Lily pulled the covers over her face and cried for her father.

Lily could hear his boots moving towards her and she lost control of her cry. She yelled for her father and mother but heard nothing back from them. They didn't hear her.

The shadow of his hand reached over her blanket, and watching it come closer sent shivers down her spine. She squeezed her bunny as tight as she could and when he pulled the blanket off of her she froze. She didn't know what to do. He pointed his gun at

Lily, but then she heard something, it was a voice, and everything went black.

"Lily. Lily? Lily! Wake up, sleepy head!"

Lily opened her eyes and saw Janet, her best friend, staring at her.

"About time. Did you forget we were getting up early?"

"Yeah, thanks for waking me up, I had that same dream again."

"Oh Lily, you're still having that dream?"

"Yeah, but this time it felt different."

"Was it because I woke you up?"

"No. Just never mind, I want to forget about it. Let me get dressed and I'll see you in a minute."

Lily and Janet went down the Grand Wailea resort elevator and started their morning tour of the island. Thinking of the blistering sun, Janet first stopped in the souvenir shop beside the hotel to buy another bottle of sunblock so they didn't fry in the heat. They shopped some more around the area for just an hour or two, then waved down a taxi to head back to the hotel to finally swim at the beach. The sky was covered with pink, orange, yellow, and blue layered clouds. The ocean was as blue as sapphires and so clear you could see every pebble and shell lying in the sand.

Afterwards, Lily and Janet stopped by a different gift shop near the hotel for more souvenirs. After browsing, they went back to their room to swim in the pool outside on the balcony.

"Hey Lily, can you throw me the purple donut?"

"Ya, give me a second."

Lily laid her magazine on the table and walked over to the door to grab the float that was lying on the ground already pumped up and ready to use.

"Here ya go."

"Thanks! Hey Lily, what do you want to do next on our last day?"

"I don't know? Maybe we can take that boat ride that guy and his wife offered us. What was his name Aiden?"

"No, it was Allen."

"Oh, yeah, that's right. I can call him and see if he and his wife want to have dinner around six thirty," Lily suggested.

"Yeah, that sounds fun. If they aren't available, we can shop some more, or I heard they are shooting off fireworks by the beach further downtown."

Right after they discussed it, the phone began to ring. It was resting on a beautiful glass coffee table, with coral-colored seahorse table legs, beside the pool.

"Huh, maybe they were already going to invite us," Janet chuckled.

Janet picked up the phone and answered.

"Hello?"

"Hi' my name is James Cowell, are you Lily Davis?"

"No' this is her friend, hold on."

She took the phone away from her face and turned to Lily.

"Hey Lily, there's a man on the phone who wants to talk with you."

"A man?"

"Ya, he sounds hot and like he could be around twenty-five. You should save the number for me."

Janet passed the phone to Lily with a smile, and Lily walked away from the pool laughing at her comment.

"Hello?"

"Hi, are you Lily Davis?"

"Yes, who might this be?"

"My name is James Cowell, I'm calling from the police department of Harpswell Maine. I called to talk to you about your father."

Lily didn't like the tone of the man's voice and started to panic.

"What? What about my father?"

"Well, I'm sorry to tell you, but your father passed away. He died in his sleep last night. We are arranging a funeral for him in two days," said the man over the phone in a more softened tone.

Lily's vision went blurry from the tears forming in her eyes. She couldn't believe what the man had just told her over the phone. The news of her father struck her like a bullet, and she suddenly felt cold and dizzy. Lily's knees gave out, and she collapsed to the ground sobbing, still holding the phone in her hand. She cried for a minute, but then gave herself a few seconds to gather her words after falling into a chair. Janet saw her bawling and jumped out of the pool immediately. She didn't know why Lily was upset, but comforted her with a hug and then jumped back in the pool to give her some space. Lily then took a deep breath so that she could talk to the man on the other side of the phone.

"I'm sorry miss. I'm sure you'll be coming down for his funeral?"

Lily cleared her throat to give the man an answer, "Yes, uh… I will leave today and I'll be there."

"Ok great, and, again, I'm sorry for your loss. Your father was a good man and he did a lot for the town."

"Yes, yes he was. I'll come down and you said the funeral was on the twenty-seventh?"

"Yes."

"Ok, I'll pack and head out right away. Will I see you at the funeral?"

"Yes, I'll be there, thank you for contacting me." Lily put the phone on the glass coffee table by the pool and wiped the wet lines on her face.

"What happened Lily?"

"That was the police," Lily paused for a second. "My father passed away last night."

"Oh Lily, I'm so sorry. Are you going up there?"

"Yes."

"When are you going?"

"I need to pack and leave today. I know this is all very unexpected but I want to ask if you will come with me? I would love some company and I need some support. My father and I were seriously close. I haven't seen him in a good year, so I should be there and say goodbye one last time. Please Janet," Lily begged.

"Of course I will."

"Thank you. We'll have to pack up and leave soon because the funeral is on the twenty-seventh and I want to get there a little sooner to clean out the house and grab some stuff."

"I'm guessing it takes about eight hours to get there from here right?" Janet added the hours in her head and thought of the time difference.

"Well, close, five hours. We have to get a flight booked quickly. Hopefully they have a flight going out today." Janet called the airport and asked the lady if any flights were going out to Maine. "They have one going out at seven am and a flight going out at nine pm."

"Ok, well, nine o'clock is too late. We would arrive around seven in the morning. We'll have to book the seven o'clock flight. So, with the time difference, Hawaii is about five hours behind Maine so we would get there at five in the afternoon. We're going to have to pack quickly, that only gives us about under an hour."

"Ok, so I'll pack our things and you go down to the lobby and say we're leaving early," Said Janet.

"Ok, I'll be back in a few minutes and I'll book the flight too."

Lily walked away from the pool, out of her hotel room, and took the elevator down to the front desk.

The elevator opened and Lily went to the front desk and saw no one there. It was six in the morning, so Lily thought she would see at least one employee.

She went to the front desk bell and pressed it twice. After a minute or two, she saw a woman come around the corner. The woman wasn't ready for the day, she was still wearing a plush hotel robe, fuzzy red slippers, and was pulling rollers out of her hair. Lily waited until she was finished taking her rollers out and told the woman they were leaving a day early. The lady put her glasses on, put information into the computer, and gave Lily a receipt to sign. After Lily spoke with the lady and signed her receipt, She booked the seven am flight to Maine. She walked back towards the elevator and went back to their room to tell Janet about her interesting front desk experience.

She walked in and Janet was changed out of her bathing suit, packing both her and Lily's suitcase.

"We can finish packing and get something to eat before we go, then we can head over to the airport," Lily suggested.

"Ok, I'm going to dry out our bathing suit with the hairdryer the best I can. My suitcase is mostly done, I just started gathering your things. I think I put everything on your bed, but I know for sure your makeup bag is still in the bathroom."

"I'll grab it before I forget."

Lily walked to the bathroom and started putting her makeup, hair ties, and little bottles of shampoo from the hotel into the makeup bag. She looked up in the mirror and started thinking about her father. Lily wondered how a man in his forties died in his sleep.

Lily started to tear up again realizing that both her mom and dad were gone, she had no family to go to for Christmas, no surprise visits, no more hugs from any of them. Janet called Lily from the bedroom and asked if she needed help but told her she would be there In a second.

A single tear drop fell down her cheek but wiped it away quickly with her jacket sleeve. Lily waited for her red, wet eyes to clear before walking out of the bathroom.

Lily and Janet finished packing their suitcases and at about five forty am they waved for a taxi and left the hotel to go grab a bite to eat. They were too full to move after they ate some fast food but had to head back to the hotel to grab their luggage. Then waved for a taxi to head to the airport to fly to Maine.

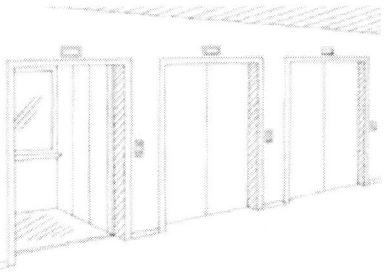

Chapter II
The Trip To Harpswell

"Hey Janet, we made it, and right on time, they are just now boarding."

Janet and Lily showed the young lady their boarding passes and seat numbers and went through the door to board the plane. They walked seven isles back passing businessmen, little kids, and families that looked like they were on their way towards a relaxing vacation.

The girls found their seats and shoved their suitcases in the compartment above them, then gladly sat down.

"These seats are nice! I thought they would be hard and not up to date like our plane to Hawaii and the trip to Connecticut," snickered Lily.

The plane seats were as soft as a fresh Georgia peach. They were navy blue with two red stripes down the middle. The walls were almost a cadet gray and the carpet was navy blue.

An older lady, old enough to be Lily's grandma, was walking her way through the aisle with a snack and beverage cart. The lady had her grayish-white hair pulled back in a low ponytail and had what looked like a brand-new navy-colored uniform on.

The woman's eyes were a beautiful misty blue and stood out because of her uniform color.

"Would you girls like anything from the cart?"

Lily looked at the cart and couldn't decide if she wanted anything. Janet on the other hand knew exactly what she wanted.

"Yes, can I have some chocolate almonds please, and tea?"

"Ok, here you go. Can I have your card miss?"

Janet gave the old lady her card and paid for her chocolate almonds and tea. The old lady thanked Janet and continued asking passengers if they needed anything. The captain had the plane flying smoothly and the sky was as blue as the ocean below. The clouds, fluffy and thick, looked as if you could jump on them.

Later on, as Janet opened her chocolate almonds, they felt something. The plane shook for a quick moment and it felt like a small earthquake. Janet's chocolate almonds fell one by one onto the carpet and Lily laughed hysterically.

"Damn, I wanted to eat those."

Everyone on the plane was confused, and people were looking around wondering if someone else on the plane knew what was going on.

"Did we hit some birds?" Janet asked herself out loud.

A noise came from the ceiling speakers, as the captain started talking on the intercom.

"Ladies and Gentleman, sorry to disturb you, but we are experiencing a small mishap and will be arriving a half an hour late. We'll be there shortly, thank you."

Janet unbuckled and got out of her seat.

"What are you doing?" Lily asked.

"I'm getting more almonds!"

"What," Janet said.

"I'm still hungry! Those little packages have more air than food in them."

Janet walked to the lady with the snack cart and told her about her incident. Janet turned around and sat down with a bag of free almonds and started to eat them out of the bag.

"I love these, they're so good. You want some Lily?"

Lily thought about her offer for a second. They looked too good to pass up. She grabbed a couple out of the bag and ate them promptly.

"These are good! You know what, now I'm hungry. I'm getting some too."

Lily got up and walked down the aisle to the lady and asked for three packages of chocolate almonds and a bottle of water. Just before Lily was going to give the old lady her card the plane shook and everyone jerked forward. Lily and the old lady crashed to the ground. Lily's head hit the edge of the seat hard and started to bleed. She put her index and middle finger together and pressed on her cut, hoping to not let the blood ooze out.

Lily helped the old woman off the ground and the woman thanked her. She then pulled her card out of her wallet and paid for her almonds and the bottle of water. The woman opened a first aid box under the cart and grabbed an alcohol wipe and a large band-aid. She handed it to Lily and told her to go to the bathroom to clean up. Lily did as she said, wiped off the blood and placed the band-aid on her forehead.

She tossed the wrapper in the trash and returned to her seat. Lily buckled her seat belt and rubbed her head hoping to make the pain go away.

"Oh my God, Lily, are you alright?"

"Yeah, I'm good. My head hurts a little, but I can take something for it later."

"Ok. Hey, something has to be wrong with this plane. I mean that was a big jolt," Janet said concerned.

Just after, the captain spoke on the intercom and apologized for the mishap. He said they were arriving in ten minutes and not to panic, but after that fall, Lily didn't feel like being calm. The captain had announced that there was a problem with one of the engines and assured everyone that they would land in time to evacuate the plane.

The captain informed the passengers that he had called the airport on his radio asking for help. Suddenly everybody started talking about what the captain had said and felt somewhat relieved. A little girl around the age of four started to bawl, and a man across from Lily and Janet was sweating bullets looking out his window, wondering how far they were from the runway. The man then noticed the engine on the wing was on fire. His wife next to him started screaming and yelling that they were all going to die. Three flight attendants came out from the back of the plane and started to tell people to calm down. One of the women went to the front of the plane and started telling people what they were going to do when they landed, in case of an emergency landing.

The woman told all the passengers that they would be taking the evacuation slide as soon as they landed in an orderly fashion line if the captain said it was dangerous. Lily and Janet stayed calm and distracted themselves by talking until they landed.

She would've never thought she would be on a plane that had caught fire. Lily opened her chocolate almonds and popped a couple in her mouth to settle her nerves.

"Yeah, these are so good. I know what I'm getting on the flight back," She nervously commented to Janet.

They were five minutes away from landing, and Janet looked out the man's window across from her and Lily's seat observing the fire. She saw darker smoke blowing endlessly from the engine.

"I hope we land this plane soon. I don't like how that smoke looks."

The captain came on the speakers and announced their arrival would be in three minutes and that everyone would have to do an emergency evacuation.

Janet looked out the window again and the smoke was getting worse. Dread filled her as the smoke got thicker and thicker. Finally, Janet looked out her window and could see part of the airport and instantly was filled with relief.

"Look Lily, we made it!"

The plane lowered closer to the ground, and everyone started getting ready to get off the plane. Bump, bump, bump! They were now thankfully on the ground. The captain came out of the cockpit and told all the passengers to exit the plane calmly but quickly.

Janet and Lily grabbed their carry-on bags and purse and stood up out of their seats. They stood in line, slowly stepping closer to exit the emergency slide. Lily looked over and couldn't see out of the windows. The whole left side was filled with thick black smoke. They all needed to get off quickly. Lily and Janet were finally at the exit chute and went down together simultaneously.

They slid down the long wide slide and before they knew it their feet were on the ground. Two men with orange vests led Janet, Lily, and a boy behind them away from the plane into the small crowd of passengers and crew. Three fire trucks pulled up to the left side of the airplane and men came out of the truck, running to grab the supply line hoses out from the trucks. The brave men sprayed water on the destroyed engine, forcing the fire to go out slowly. Everyone was safely off the plane watching the firefighters put out the fire.

Forty minutes later the fire was out and they checked the plane. Firefighters said it was safe for the workers to grab all the bags off the plane and all carry-on bags that were not grabbed.

"Wow, I don't know if I could stand staying on that plane any longer, what an experience," Janet joked.

"I know, that was terrifying. I don't think we're going to take that airline back to California."

They both laughed and followed the other passengers to the baggage claim. They safely brought all the luggage out of the plane and sent it inside. Lily and Janet found their bags, walked through the airport to the front doors and Janet waved for a taxi.

A taxi pulled up and the driver put their luggage in the trunk.

"400 West on Roxbury Street please."

The taxi driver started to head to Lily's house, but they would arrive at the house a little later than planned. The ride was a good twenty minutes because the driver passed the wrong road and had to turn around. Lily directed the wrinkled man to the right road and the right house, and they finally arrived after their long scary experience. An experience they wouldn't forget.

"Finally! I know I'll sleep well tonight after that morning," Janet remarked.

Lily paid the driver and thanked him. He opened the trunk and put their suitcases on the sidewalk next to Lily and Janet. The driver drove off and the girls walked up the steps of Lily's father's old brick house excited, and glad to be there. But, little did they know, something would be coming for them by being in Harpswell Maine. Their lives would change forever from this point on.

Chapter III
The House

"Wow, Lily, your father's house is big."

"Ya, we had good memories here. My father worked very hard throughout his life. He was a gold and silver miner for about thirty years. He loved his money, was a good miner, and was always getting lucky."

Janet reached for the door handle and tried opening the door.

"It's locked."

"I knew it would be. James, the cop from earlier, called me before we left Hawaii and said he made sure it was locked. I told him I knew where the spare key was."

Lily bent down in front of a dog statue beside the door. She tilted it up and there was a key underneath.

"He always kept a key under here."

Lily gave Janet the key to open the door and they looked inside. The living room had endless piles of boxes and random stuff on the wooden floors. Lily was shocked to see such a mess in her father's house. Janet's mouth was open so wide a black-capped chickadee could fly in. Janet shut the door and they carefully stepped over the boxes Lily's father left on the dusty wooden floor. Janet and Lily put their suitcases on the chairs in the dining room and Lily poured a drink of water from the kitchen sink.

She gave Janet the glass of water, and she drank it so fast that Lily was shocked she didn't choke.

"Wow Lily, this water is good! Some people say all water tastes the same, but I don't think so."

"Ya, it depends where you are. It tastes different in different places."

"Hey, Lily. You want to start cleaning the mess in the living room and the rest of the house?"

"Ya, we can do it after I show you your room."

Lily and Janet walked up the old creaky stairs.

"Lily, your father didn't like to clean, did he?"

Lily laughed. "Yeah, he always just put something wherever and cleaned when it was necessary. But, I've never seen the house like this."

Lily opened the first door on the left. They both walked into the room and looked around. Janet was staying in a room with forest green walls and white and yellow flowers. The bedspread was silky white

24

with green pillows and on each side of the bed was a nightstand with old gray lamps.

"Oh Lily, it's beautiful, and I read at night so the lamps by the bed are nice. Thanks!"

"No problem."

"What does your room look like?"

"Well, I'll show ya, it's right across the hall."

Lily opened the door to her old room and showed Janet around. It had gray walls and the curtains were white with cobalt blue stripes. Her bed had gray sheets that were rippled, and a light purple blanket was draped at the end of the bed.

"Oh, your room is nice too. Your father has a very nice house, but it's very messy."

"I agree. We can clean a little downstairs then order something to eat."

"Yeah, sounds good. It needs a little cleaning."

Janet got a head start downstairs while Lily put her suitcase on her bed. Before she walked out she noticed a new painting hanging

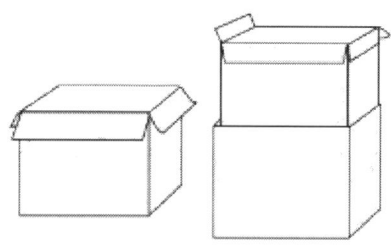

on the wall beside her dresser. It was a beautiful piece of art. Lily looked one last time at it and jogged down the stairs joining Janet. Janet found the cleaning closet and started sweeping while Lily moved some furniture around the living room.

"Wow, I didn't realize how much stuff my father had."

"Yeah, it's a little much. Do you think he went to a garage sale before he died?"

Lily chuckled. "He could have. Some of this stuff doesn't look familiar."

Lily finished moving all the furniture in the living room and Janet finished sweeping all the dust away in the kitchen and upstairs in the bedrooms.

"I think that's good for today Janet. I mean it's eight-forty,"

"Yeah, we did a lot and it already looks better in here. The windows need to be washed, but I'll do them tomorrow," Lily said, exhausted from the long day.

Lily and Janet went to the kitchen and had leftover food her father had in the fridge. They ate pickles, cheese, and salami, with white chocolate chip cookies for dessert. Then both girls went upstairs to their rooms and went to bed for the night.

Chapter IV
Interesting Findings

The next morning, Lily opened her curtains and saw the beautiful multi-colored sunrise in the sky. Then, Lily and Janet opened their doors at the same time.

"Morning."

"Morning! How'd you sleep Lily?"

"I slept like a rock. I was exhausted from using so much energy yesterday."

"Yeah, I did too. Yesterday was a lot. I feel more energized now that I got some sleep."

They both rushed downstairs and ate some morning breakfast before starting the day.

"Thanks, Lily, I didn't know you could cook so well," Janet laughed.

"Well, I'm not a chef but yeah I thought it was good. I know that biscuits and gravy recipe by heart. My grandmother and I used to cook the best biscuits and gravy with scrambled eggs and ham every morning when I visited her. She would always make the gravy and I would make the biscuits. When the biscuits were done my grandpa would snatch one or two to snack on before we even started. I eventually caught on after the third time making them, so I made extra biscuits after that."

"You need to show me how. But, do you want to pick up the living room more and I could sweep in the other bedroom?"

"Yeah, let's start doing that. I've been wanting to look in those boxes that were in the corner."

"What boxes?"

"The boxes by the fireplace."

"Oh, ok. Yeah you do that and I'll go upstairs."

Janet finished her orange juice and walked into the living room with Lily.

She grabbed the broom that she left yesterday against the wall and went upstairs to the second bedroom to sweep.

Lily looked in one of the boxes and found some of her personal items.

"Oh my god, I can't believe he still has this."

She grabbed an old pot she made in school when she was ten. It was white and had red and orange violets going up the pot. Lily put it back in the box and grabbed some papers that looked like old drawings from childhood. They were coloring pages from when she was a kid. The pages had monkeys and elephants drawn on them, and one had an ice cream cone with pink sprinkles. Drawn on another page was herself holding a green balloon, going down a slide at the playground. The last page in her hand was a drawing of herself, her parents, and her seven-year-old dog Jasper.

"I forgot I drew these."

   Lily picked up the box and went upstairs to show Janet how creative she was as a kid, and to show her what she looked like when she was younger.

"Janet, look, It's some of my childhood things."

"Oh, I want to see! Dang, Lily, you were so cute."

"Yeah right, my face looks like I smelled a fart when they took it. I mean, look at my face. I look confused or something. I don't know why they kept that picture."

Janet chuckled, "Maybe someone did fart, but the picture turned out decent. I know my mother kept just about every picture from every family event."

"Hey Lily, are there more boxes downstairs?"

"Yeah, why?"

"Maybe there's more stuff from when you were a kid. It's fun to look at old stuff from the past."

"Maybe, I don't know, let's go look. I think there's like four boxes I haven't opened yet. I wonder if my diary is in there. That would definitely be a good read."

They ran out of the room and ran downstairs to see what was in the rest of the boxes. Janet looked in two and Lily took the other two. Janet found a bunch of old books Lily's father used to read at night, and some pictures in an album book. Lily also found some books in one box with a bag of marbles and some old toys. The other box had some small glass jars wrapped in newspapers, a picture of Lily, her mother, and her father, and a few more items.

"What's that Lily?"

"It's a picture of me and my parents. I think we took it like nine years ago at the ice cream parlor."

"You should put it up on the fireplace next to that lion statue," Janet suggested.

"Yeah, I think I should. It shouldn't be in this box. It's one of my favorite pictures of us together."

Lily walked over to the fireplace and put it next to a purple vase and a lion statue. She stared at the picture, then, in the corner of Lily's eyes, she saw the lion statue. She looked at the head and noticed something odd about it. The head was crooked.

"I've never noticed that before."

"Noticed what?"

   Janet stood up and walked over to the fireplace where Lily was looking at the statue.

"This lion statue's head is crooked."

"Huh, that's weird. It doesn't look like it's supposed to be like that. Lily, how is it staying on?"

"I don't know. If it was broken it wouldn't be staying there like that."

   Lily reached and put her hand on the head of the statue turning it clockwise.

 "It turns, and did you hear that?"

"Yeah, it sounded like something clicked."

"Yep, and it felt like the fireplace shifted when I moved the head."

"Oh My god, Lily! What if it's one of those hidden rooms."

"No. I grew up here and I know there isn't a secret room. But, that would be cool."

"Well, try moving it again."

"Alright, but I don't think anything is going to appear."

Lily turned the lion's head back to the left, then something happened, something incredible. Lily was shocked. She couldn't believe what her eyes were seeing. Janet's jaw dropped and then she jumped up and down.

"I told you Lily! Wow, unbelievable."

Lily was shocked. She never knew about the door that led to the hidden room behind the fireplace.

Chapter V
Beyond The Wall

They both peeked through the side of the fireplace opening and walked into the big square room. Janet found the light switch and flipped it on. Lily and Janet's eyes were both wide open.

"Your father has a secret room, THAT IS SO COOL!"

"I had no idea this was here." Lily paused. "I wonder why it's hidden, and why he never told me about it."

"Maybe it's to hide all his valuables, or he just wanted his privacy."

They looked around. There were books by a green old-fashioned chair and a standing globe beside the table. The carpet was darker red and there were beautiful paintings on the walls. One painting was of a pirate ship hung above a chair. One had a river flowing through a big forest. There was a desk across from the table that Lily was looking at. Lily walked over to where Janet was and saw another painting. A painting of her dad.

Janet was going through papers that were spread out on the desk. As Janet was looking through the papers she saw a letter, a letter with Lily's name on it taped to the desk.

"Hey Lily, there's a letter with your name on it. I'm assuming your father wrote it."

Lily walked over to the desk and picked up the letter.

"A letter for me?"

She tore it open and when she saw the date in the corner she looked at Janet confused. It said, August 24th, 1987.

"Janet, this letter was written a couple of days ago!"

She unfolded the letter and started to read what her father had written.

"Dear Lily,

I love you so very much. I have been waiting for you to discover the room that I have here. I wrote this letter for you to find what I've left behind. I want no one else to have it. I've saved it for years. But someone is watching and they will do anything to get it. I made clues so you could find them. I know you can solve them because you are very smart, my girl. Keep these clues safe and let no one else read them. Don't trust anyone and stay safe. I love you, baby, so much.

P.s. - Take my pocket knife, you never know when you'll need it.

Love Father, *

Lily was on the verge of crying. She looked over and saw the pocket knife and a small piece of paper. It said 4786 and at the bottom below the number underlined it said to be <u>safe.</u>

"What does that mean?" Janet asked.

"I think it's a clue. The first clue."

Lily put the red pocket knife in her pocket.

"Maybe it's some type of code you have to type in."

"I could be, but to what?"

"Well, I saw a box with a lock on it upstairs in the guest room when I was cleaning."

"Let's go try it."

They ran out of the living room and upstairs to the bedroom where Janet was just cleaning.

"It's over here," Janet pointed.

"Huh, it does have a lock on it."

"If it opens, what do you think is in there?"

"I don't know, probably another clue."

Lily rolled the knob on the lock to put the code in. She put in all the numbers and it didn't open.

"Did you put the code in wrong?" Asked Janet

"I might've. I'll try it again."

Lily turned the knob and it still didn't open.

"I don't think this is it. It's something else. I know! My father's safe."

"His safe?"

"Yeah, he had a safe and kept stuff in there. I don't know what, but it might be in there if he still has it."

"If he still had it, where would it be?"

"Probably in the den under his desk. There's a hole under the desk he used to keep a safe in."

They went downstairs and walked into the den by the downstairs bathroom.

"I feel like I lost four pounds walking up and down these stairs."

Lily chuckled, "Yeah, me too."

Lily sat down on the floor, reached in the hole under the desk, and felt around for the safe.

"Got it. Do you want to open it, Janet?"

"Sure, what was the code again?

"Ohhh wait, the paper says be safe, and safe is underlined. The answer was there the whole time, it must be in the safe."

"Open it, then. Open it!"

"Chill out! You never told me what the code was. What is it?"

"It's 4786."

Janet quickly turned the knob and the lock clicked.

"Lily. It opened."

Janet and Lily looked in the little safe and there was a key along with another note. The key was golden brown, and the top of the key had a tree with a circle around it.

"I like the key," Janet said.

"Yeah, it's gorgeous, is that another clue?"

"It looks like it."

Lily read the piece of paper.

It says, "Go to the place where we had our summer picnics. Look for the clue by our names." *

Lily thought for a moment, then realized it was easy.

"I know where to find the next clue. We used to go to Clover Lake to have picnics all the time."

"I guess that's where we're going," said Janet.

Lily grabbed the key to the house, the clues, and the keys to her father's car. Then opened the garage door and unlocked the car.

"You want to drive Janet?"

"No, you can, I'll study the clues more."

Janet sat in the passenger seat and Lily started the car. She put it in reverse and drove out of the garage and drove into town. Past the town was where the lake was, and the coffee shop on the way caught Janet's eye.

"Oh, we should check out the coffee shop after we find the next clue. I would die for a cappuccino," said Janet.

"Yeah, we can do that, I'm kind of thirsty too. Did you find anything?"

"Well, it says to look for the clue by our names. What does that mean?"

"I believe it means to look by the old oak tree. My father carved our names in the tree years ago. Maybe he carved something else next to our names."

"Well, we'll find out. I also noticed at the end of every clue there is a star."

"Good observation, I didn't notice that."

   It took a good ten minutes to drive to Clover Lake. They pulled up by a hill and parked the brick-red car in the parking lot. They stepped out of the car and started their journey up the hill toward the lake.

Chapter VI

Clover Lake

Lily pointed. "The Lake is hidden behind this hill."

They walked up the hill and looked around.

"There it is, Clover Lake."

They walked down the hill until they reached the edge of the long lake.

"Oh, this is a nice lake, and I love the location. It's peaceful out here."

"This is the tree."

"Oh, I see your names."

Janet read out loud the names that were carved into the tree. "Lily, Amber, and Josh Davis, July 1st, 1978. 1978, so you were like eleven when your dad carved this?"

"Yeah, it was a long time ago. I still remember it like it was yesterday. It was one of my favorite summers. The sun was shining and there were no clouds in sight. My mother would make ham and cheese sandwiches and oatmeal raisin cookies, and all kinds of stuff. She liked making big picnics. We would put the traditional plaid blanket down on the grass and eat under the old oak tree. We told each other what we saw in the clouds and what animals we saw by the pond. There were ducks in the pond, fish jumping out of the water, geese always flying over the lake, all kinds of frogs, and of course crickets. I remember eating the biggest watermelon slice from the basket, and my father stood up from the blanket and started carving our names in the tree. He told me it would be there forever and I could always look at it to remember that day."

"That sounds nice. You had a fun childhood here."

Lily and Janet sat on the tall grass next to the tree facing toward the lake to see the beautiful country view. Swans were ducking their heads under the water and fish jumped out as if they could fly. Then they got up and looked around the tree for more carvings her father may have made for their next clue.

"Lily, I don't think he carved the clue in the tree."

"I don't see anything either. Try looking on the ground, maybe he buried it."

Lily walked closer to the lake and began looking on the ground, in the bushes, and the tall grass to see if anything was there. Janet looked at the ground around the tree and saw nothing. They looked for about five minutes and found nothing. Lily and

Janet met back at the tree and sat down. They sat there for a few minutes thinking about the poem, and wondering if they missed something important in the last clue.

Sitting there for a while, she started playing with blades of grass hoping it would help her think of an idea. She then looked over and saw something in the corner of her eye. A good-sized hole was under the tree, hidden from the tall overgrown grass.

"Hey, there's a hole here under these tree roots."

Janet leaned over and saw the small hole Lily described. Lily sat closer and pulled chunks of grass out of the way so she could get a better view of the inside. She saw something brown inside. Lily reached her hand in the hole and felt something cubed. It scared her for a second, but she quickly realized it was the next clue.

"Janet, it's a box, this has to be it!"

"Pull it out!"

"I can't, it's stuck, the roots are in the way. How did he get this in here?"

"Lily, your knife, pull out your knife."

"Oh, yeah, that will work. It might take me a minute to cut through."

Excitement filled the air as the girls were both rushing to open the mysterious box that was left under the tree. She pulled out her knife and started to cut the roots. It took a while to cut and Janet had to take over for a second to give Lily a break. The roots were thicker than they thought and Lily grabbed the knife and started cutting again. Finally, she cut the last root, she pulled the box out of the hole, and wiped the dirt off the top.

"That's a cool box! He definitely hid it well. It took us a good while to find it."

The box was more on the rectangle side when they pulled it out. Lily wiped it off more and could see some writing on the top.

"The box has my name on it."

"It does! He probably put it on there so if someone found it they would know who it belonged to."

The box had a keyhole and they figured that was what the key they found earlier was for. Janet gave her the key and Lily placed it in the keyhole, hoping it was the right one.

"It opened!"

Inside, there was a long piece of paper in the box.

"Is this another poem?"

"Yeah, I think so, and look, it has a star at the end."

Lily licked her lips and read the words that were written on the small paper.

*"This next clue is hard to find, Look harder past the words I write. It's been a good life, but now I must go. Find the next clue below her in Adams Grove. * "*

"What does my father mean by this?"

They both looked at the note and tried to think of any locations that came to mind.

"I don't know what the clue means. We can figure this out later. Hey, I'm getting a little thirsty, you want to get some coffee back in town and we can talk about it there?"

"Yeah, sounds good, I could definitely go for something." Janet helped Lily up off the ground and grabbed the box to take back to the car.

Chapter VII
Men In The Coffee Shop

Lily took a look around the lake for the last time and started walking back to her dad's car with Janet. Lily put the clue in her pocket while looking for the keys to the car, but realized the keys weren't in her pocket. She searched her other pocket and started to panic.

"Do you have the keys, Janet?"

"Yeah, you dropped them earlier back at the tree and I got distracted."

Janet reached into her pocket, grabbed the keys, and threw them to Lily.

"Catch."

"Thanks, and nice throw too."

Lily unlocked the car and put the keys in the ignition. They drove a few miles back towards town and looked for the coffee shop.

"Oh, there it is. It felt further than this!"

Lily parked the car in the back row where there were only a couple of cars. The brick building was decent-sized. There were murals of coffee cups, muffins, and names of the people who worked there over the years. Janet always had a passion for art. Just one piece told multiple emotions, moods, and stories.

"Someone has a good talent and a creative mind. I love this!"

"Yeah, it's been repainted. It looks a lot better now. They add new names all the time and you know what is really cool?"

"What?"

"I used to work here too, before my mom died. Look."

Lily pointed to her right, and there was her name, written in black paint.

"Ok, that is neat."

Lily and Janet then walked around the building and went inside. There were different colored seats and the tables were wooden with a darker wood stain, giving the shop an authentic charm.

"It's so cute in here! I love their choice of decorations."

"Yeah, it's my favorite coffee shop, nothing like this is in California. And, I've always been in love with the ceiling lights."

They walked to a sage green booth and sat down. A teenage boy, about sixteen, grabbed them small menus and went to get the waiter. "Yes, I love this booth. It's one of my favorite colors."

"I'm more of a dark navy blue or royal blue person, but green is cool too. What are you getting Lily?"

"I have no idea. Everything looks tasty. I think I'll go with my usual strawberry smoothie."

A young woman came to the table and pulled out her small notepad.

"Hi, my name is Adriana and I'm going to be serving you guys today. Have either of you guys decided what you would like to order?"

"Yes, I would like a strawberry smoothie with whipped cream please," said Lily.

"And for you, miss?"

"Uh, I think I will take a white caramel chocolate mocha with whipped cream."

"Ok, they should be ready in five minutes."

"Thank you!"

Janet and Lily handed their menus to the waitress and talked about the next clue while they waited for their drinks. Lily pulled the next clue out of her pocket and read it out loud.

"This next clue is hard to find, Look harder past the words I write. It's been a good life, but now I must go. Find the next clue below her in Adams Grove. *"

"I don't know what that means, and what's Adams Grove?" Janet asked.

"I'm not sure. I think that's the first thing we need to find out."

The waitress came back from the counter with the drinks and put the tray on the table. Lily and Janet grabbed their drinks, and the woman gave them straws before taking the tray off the table

"One smoothie, and one white Caramel chocolate mocha with whipped cream."

"Thank you."

"Anything else for you girls?"

"No, I think we're good," Lily replied back.

"Ok, here is your bill, Miss?"

"Davis," said Lily.

"Did you say Davis? You're not related to Josh Davis, are you?"

"Actually, yes, he was my father."

"Oh, I'm so sorry for your loss. He was a great man. He used to come in here every Saturday and order coffee and a blueberry muffin. Well, here you go, Miss Davis, have a wonderful day."

"You too, thank you."

　The waitress walked away and started cleaning the table behind Lily and Janet. The bell above the front door rang and three men walked into the building. One man looked about forty-five and was wearing a black tux and had dark brown hair. The two other men looked to be in their twenties and had leather jackets on with t-shirts, and blue jeans. One had brown hair and the other had black hair. Lily looked at the men and couldn't help but wonder what they were up to. They looked serious, and to Lily, they looked like they were up to no good.

　The men walked over to the tables and they all sat at the table across from Lily and Janet's. Lily tried not to look at the men, but she had a feeling their eyes were fixated on her. She glanced over, and she was right. The man with the tux was staring intensely. Their eyes locked for just a second before she looked away, but it felt longer than a second. His eyes were intense, and she felt as if she was being examined. His right eye was a greenish-yellow color and the other was a dark gray almost black. Janet reached out and gave Lily a spoon to scoop out her cherries, making Lily focus back on her drink.

"You good, Lily?"

"Those men look like trouble."

"Yeah, they do. Let's look at the clue," Janet suggested.

Lily ate a cherry on top of her smoothie, sipped the cold beverage up her straw, and focused on the next clue they found.

"So, I think Adams Grove is a place, but I've never heard of it."

"We could ask around town."

"No," Lily snapped. "Remember what my father said in his first note. He said don't trust anyone."

Janet drank her coffee and whipped cream stuck to her lip.

"That's true. Well, how about the waitress? She seems trustworthy."

"Yeah, we can ask her. She wouldn't say anything."

The woman walked past Lily and Janet's table with two dirty glasses and a stack of plates on a tray.

"Hey, mis? We have a question for you."

"Sure, how can I help?"

"Well, do you know where Adams Grove is?" Janet asked.

"Yeah, it's the cemetery. You know Harrison's barber shop in town? It's the back road behind it. Just go straight and it's about two miles down."

"Wait, I thought that was a Periton cemetery?"

"It was, but they changed the name a couple of months ago."

"Well, thank you."

Adriana left and walked to the back of the building to wash the dirty dishes she just picked up.

"That cemetery is where my mom was buried, and the officer over the phone said my dad's funeral is being held there."

"The paper said under her. I hope we ain't digging anyone up." Lily laughed.

"I hope not either. Hey, did you notice those two men seemed a little interested in what we had to say," Lily whispered.

"Yeah, I saw that too! They keep looking over here and then discussing something."

"Maybe we should discuss it in the car."

"Good idea. I'm ready anyway."

Janet and Lily walked out of the coffee shop and got into the car. Lily put the key in the ignition, backed up and they drove out of the parking lot.

"So, the next clue is in Adam Grove cemetery. Do you want to check out the cemetery today or tomorrow?"

"What time is it?"

Lily looked at her watch and read the time.

"It's 2:46, and it gets dark around six here."

"Yeah, let's head to the cemetery and check it out. I think I know exactly where to look too."

Lily already started driving towards town and, before she could drive half a mile, she saw something in her car mirror.

Chapter VIII
Unknown Followers

It was a black Mercedes.

"Hey Janet, does that Mercedes behind us look familiar to you?"

Janet looked in her side mirror.

"Yeah, it does. I swear I saw that somewhere."

"It's going a little fast, don't you think? I'm going thirty-five through here and he's riding my tail."

"Press on your brake. Maybe it will teach him a lesson."

"No, I don't think that's a good idea. He's not slowing down and he could run into us."

Lily looked at her mirror again and started to panic. The car was getting closer.

"I'm going to turn down this road. He's going too fast."

Lily turned and the Mercedes followed.

"Why is he following us?"

"I don't know, but I'm turning on another road.

"Maybe I can lose him."

Lily turned down another road and the Mercedes was still following them, but it was going even faster.

"LILY! I know where I've seen that car."

"Where?"

"At the coffee shop, it was two cars over from where we parked. I saw the car when you pulled out."

"Really?"

"I'm guessing it belongs to those weird men that sat at the table across from us in the coffee shop."

"Yeah, they were acting a little strange, like they were listening to our conversations."

"I'll try to lose them and go on the main street. There's usually a lot of traffic around there."

"Lily, I'm calling the police, maybe they'll send someone out here to arrest this creep."

Janet dialed 911 and waited for someone to answer.

"Hi, I would like to report what looks like a black Mercedes. He's chasing us around town. We're heading towards the main street right now because we thought we could lose them there," Janet said in a quick tone.

"Ok, well send someone out your way," the lady said over the phone.

"Thank you! They're going to send someone out near our location, and she said to make sure you don't go straight home because who knows why he's chasing us."

"Well, we're almost on Main Street."

Lily turned down one more road and the Mercedes did the same. Lily looked closely in her mirror trying to see the people in the vehicle behind them. She couldn't see the driver fully. Lily lifted her foot off the pedal and the Mercedes backed off for only a second. Lily was about to turn down the main street when the Mercedes sped up and hit Lily's bumper. Janet and Lily jerked forward, causing the car to swerve and almost hit another car.

There were so many cars here. They could for sure lose the car behind them. Lily passed three cars and turned down two more roads and the Mercedes was already losing them.

"I don't see them behind us anymore. I'm heading back to the house. We'll have to stay home and figure out the clue tomorrow after the funeral."

Lily took a back road to get them back home. It took a little longer, but was much safer, and they could slip away from the car chasing them. Lily checked to see if anyone was behind her before she pulled into the driveway. She pulled into the garage and shut off the car. As the garage shut they rushed inside to make sure all the doors were locked.

"Wow, that was a fun trip home."

"Yeah, what did they want?"

"I don't know, but they acted like they wanted to hurt us. Or maybe they wanted something."

"Let's get it off our minds, what do you want for dinner?"

"Does pizza sound good?"

"Yeah, supreme with cheese dip and breadsticks."

"Ok, I'll order it while you take your shower and we can watch a movie in my room."

"Sounds good. I'll come down when I'm done, and Lily, when the pizza guy comes, make sure he doesn't look like he wants to kill us."

Lily laughed and Janet made her way up the stairs. While Janet was taking her shower, Lily ordered the pizza and went into the hidden room to look over all the clues. Fifteen minutes later, Janet came down the stairs looking for Lily.

"Lily, where are you?"

"I'm behind the fireplace!" Lily shouted back.

Janet walked into the small study and stood behind Lily.

"What have you been up to?"

"I'm checking out these clues, but the pizza guy should be here any minute."

Right after they mentioned the pizza man, there was a knock on the door. "Oh, perfect timing. I'm starving!"

Lily sped out of the study and grabbed her wallet from the kitchen table. "It's my treat tonight."

"Alright, but tomorrow I'm buying."

Lily opened the door to see a teenage boy wearing a red and white striped long-sleeve shirt and blue jeans. He had wavy brown hair and black glasses. He gave Janet the pizzas and Lily a paper to sign for payment.

"That will be $22.50."

Lily looked in her wallet and then gave him the cash.

"Nice tip, you ladies have a good evening."

"No problem! You too."

She shut the front door and walked over to the table where Janet was already dipping a crispy golden brown breadstick into garlic sauce.

"He kind of looked like Waldo in that striped shirt," Janet remarked.

"Yeah, he had the same clothes and the same color glasses. Do you want a mellow yellow, water, or a crystal Pepsi?"

"I'll take a Mello Yello."

"Ok, catch."

Lily threw the pop can and it missed Janet's hands. The can fell on the floor and burst open spraying everywhere!

"Well, I guess I'll take another."

They both laughed and had to clean the mess before going upstairs.

"What show do you want to watch?"

Lily picked up the remote and started searching for a show.

"Well, tonight we have 'Murder She Wrote', 'The Cosby Show', 'Golden Girls', or 'Full House'."

"Ummm, 'Full House' is good, but I'm kinda feeling 'Murder She Wrote'," replied Janet.

"Yeah, I agree, Angela Lansbury is a great actress. I enjoy watching her." Lily clicked on the show and Janet pulled the covers over her and Lily.

"Oh, this episode is 'Night Fears'. It's a good one!"

Just as the episode began, the phone started to ring on the nightstand next to the bed. Lily grabbed the remote and turned down the volume to hear the phone better. She put the phone up to her ear and could hear a man talking on the other side of the line.

"Who is it?" asked Janet.

"It's a man!"

Janet came closer to listen to the call.

"I want your father's gold. Where is it?"

Lily scrunched her face and gave Janet a concerned look.

"What gold? I don't know what you're talking about?"

"If you don't tell me where it is, you and your friend are going to regret it."

"Excuse me, I'm sorry, but I don't know what you mean. Who is this?"

The man hung up the phone, and Lily turned to Janet.

"Wow, did you hear that? Who the heck was that man?"

"I don't know. He didn't sound familiar to me. I think we should be careful whenever we go out. We've had a strange day."

"Whoever that was, he was no friend to us. Why did he keep saying he wanted your father's gold? Wait, Lily, what if that's what your father left for us to find? You said he was a gold and silver miner. What if he found gold and hid it so no one could find it!"

"Janet, you might be onto something. That would explain the Mercedes chasing us around town. Someone found out. We have to be more careful from now on, and we must find what he hid before they do, if it is really gold."

"Well, tomorrow we can find the next clue and be one step closer. But, for now, let's watch the show and eat pizza."

   Lily picked up her plate and turned up the volume. They watched two episodes and around ten-thirty they went to bed. The sky that night was elegant, and many stars appeared. They were gleaming, glittering, and scattered like moondust in the sky. The moon was a mix of white and yellow like a block of colby jack cheese, surrounded by an ethereal glow. Light shines right through Lily's window and covers the floors and walls in a white ghostly cast.

It was quiet in the neighborhood, but almost too quiet. You could hear the neighborhood cats getting into the trash cans across the road, and the owls whistling and hooting, hunting for small insects to eat. It was a pleasant, calm night until they heard a car door slam in the driveway.

Janet and Lily woke up immediately, at the same time, from the noise they just heard outside. Both girls looked at each other with confusion and wondered if it was the neighbor or someone in the driveway.

"Was that a car door?"

"Yeah, but we aren't expecting company are we?"

"No, and definitely not at this hour."

Lily rolled over and reached for her watch on the nightstand beside her. "It's one-twenty-five in the morning. Who's up this late?"

Lily rolled back over and they both listened. It was silent at first, then they heard footsteps outside. Lily and Janet jumped out of bed and started walking towards the window at a slow pace. BANG, BANG, BANG! Bullets shot through the bedroom window, and glass shattered everywhere all over the floor.

Lily and Janet dropped to the floor quickly and crawled over to the bed, away from the window. The gunshots startled them, and their hearts were pumping fast from the shock. Lily's feet were cold and her body was frozen on the ground, sending a shiver down her spine. When the coast seemed clear they pushed themselves off the floor and sat back in bed. They waited a minute just sitting quietly and making sure it was safe, before moving another inch.

Janet's voice quivered, "Lily someone's trying to kill us."

"I think it's those men. I'm going to see if I'm right."

"NO, Lily, you don't know if they're still out there!"

"I'm just going to peek out the side of the window."

It was risky, but Lily walked over to the window, shaking with every step she took. She peeked out and couldn't believe what she saw. The door slammed shut and the car started to drive down the road.

"OH MY GOD! It's the Black Mercedes we saw earlier!"

"Are you sure?"

"Yes, I'm sure! I'm not blind."

"We should call the police and have them come out here."

"I'll call them. I bet the neighbors had the same idea."

Janet called the cops and they both went downstairs to discuss what had just happened.

"I know whoever called us earlier was the guy driving the Mercedes, and we know the Mercedes was at Quick Brew. It has to be those men that were sitting across from us at the coffee shop."

"I think so, too. I'm still confused about how they think your father hid gold."

"I am, too. They have to know something we don't. I think they knew my dad."

"Yeah, how else would they know anything?"

Lily thought about everything that happened that morning and couldn't put it together. There's more to this puzzle that she doesn't know about, something she's missing. Janet looked over at the window by the front door and saw the police pull up in her driveway.

"Lily, the police are here."

"Good, maybe they can track down these guys."

Lily and Janet walked over to the front door and opened it. When Lily saw the two cops at the door she immediately noticed how handsome the sergeant was. He was around Lily's age, his dark brown hair looked shiny and soft, and his bright blue eyes complemented his fair white skin. Above all was his frame and his stature. He was muscular, and his broad shoulders showed well under his tight uniform. Lily couldn't stop staring at him. She greeted him with a smile, and in return he smiled back.

"Hi, are you Lily Davis?"

Lily didn't hear the woman's question. She was too busy admiring the handsome Sergeant standing next to her in the doorway.

"Sorry, what?"

"Are you Lily Davis?" The cop repeated.

"Oh, yes, my friend called about a man in a black Mercedes."

"Yes, I'm Officer Abby Cannon and this is Sargent Owen Jackson. Can we look upstairs and check those bullets?"

"Yes, it's the first room on the right."

The cops walked in and Lily shut the front door. They all walked into the bedroom and the officers went over to the wall where the bullets were. They pulled out one of the bullets and examined it.

"Looks like this guy used a Ruger 380 pistol," said Sergeant Jackson.

"Are you sure it was a black Mercedes?"

"Yes, I saw it drive away from the house. And the same car was chasing us around town yesterday afternoon. Then, we had a weird call around nine-thirty. A man threatened us and then hung up."

"Ok, you both were definitely targeted by someone. Do you have any clue why."

The Sergeant looked out of the window and then turned to Lily.

"Where are you girls from?"

"I used to live here, but we both live in California now."

"Oh, ok, you seeing family?"

"Actually, my father just passed and we're here for his funeral tomorrow," Lily said, holding back tears.

"I'm sorry, I didn't know that, I'm sure he was a great man. I just moved here three months ago, so I don't know very many folks. But, we will look into this and get back to you if we hear any news or find anything."

"Ok, that sounds good. Thank you, Sergeant."

"No problem."

He smiled at Lily and Janet could tell she was sweet on him. The cops took the bullets, put it in the evidence bag, walked downstairs and out the door. They drove away and Janet locked the door.

"Well, this has been a nice start to the morning," said Lily.

"Yeah, I wonder what's gonna happen next, and that Sergeant was cute," Janet said with a smile.

Lily looked at Janet after she mentioned the sergeant.

"Yeah, he was cute."

"So, you're going to ask him if he has a girlfriend?"

"No, I can't do that, besides we leave in a few days."

"Well, I think it would be a good idea. He looked at you a few times and smiled. Well, I'm going back to bed for a little bit."

"I think the funeral is at 11:00 so we can sleep in a little."

"Oh, I'm definitely sleeping in. In the morning, we can search for the next clue after the ceremony."

They both walked back up the stairs and slipped back into bed. The next morning they woke up, began to get ready, and walked downstairs for breakfast.

"Hey Lily, you want cereal or eggs? I'm gonna eat cereal."

"I'll have cereal too, and we have to leave soon so we can get there early."

"Ok."

Janet tossed Lily the cereal box and Lily got a bowl and a spoon. They ate their cereal and washed the dishes when they finished. After they were done Lily went upstairs to get her purse while Janet was cleaning up the pizza box from the pizza last night. Lily came back down and opened the door to the garage.

"Are you ready to go?"

"Yeah, give me a second, I can't get this pizza box in the trash can."

"Janet, maybe try folding it like a hot dog."

"Yeah, that would probably make more sense."

Janet folded the pizza box and shoved it into the trash.

"Wow. Why didn't I think of that before?"

Lily laughed and they both walked out the door and sat in the car.

"Lily, are you sure you want to go?"

"Yeah, I have to tell him goodbye one last time."

Lily started the car, opened the garage door, and backed out of the driveway. She drove down Perry Road for a good five minutes. It was a road full of potholes, bumps, and too many hills to count. In Lily's mind, she was thinking about her father and how she'll be seeing him for the first time in a while. Janet was looking out the window staring down at the road picturing a corpse falling out of the hearse because of how bumpy it was. Then she sat up and drank some water that she brought from the house. Lily put her turn signal on and turned into the parking lot.

Chapter IX
The Funeral

It was eleven am in the morning when Lily and Janet arrived at the cemetery. It was a gorgeous morning, the sky was so open and clear, not a cloud in sight. Lily drove around the parking lot looking for a parking spot. She went around two times and then found an open spot by the right-side corner of the parking lot.

"Lily, your dad must've known a lot of people. There are so many cars here."

"Yeah, he knew everyone, he's lived here his whole life. When I was a kid I would wonder how he remembered everyone's names."

The girls stepped out of the car and locked it before joining the ceremony. They walked towards the crowd of people around the beverage and snack tables the church put out. Janet grabbed two plastic cups and poured pink lemonade from a pitcher. She walked towards Lily and handed her a cup. Officer Cowell, the cop who called Lily two days ago, came up from behind Lily and started talking to her about her father.

The reverend then saw Lily and walked over and spoke with her for a couple of minutes before Lily gave her speech. He was very loquacious because he had been talking for seven minutes. The reverend finally walked over to the casket and asked loudly for everybody to gather around and to take a seat. He began to talk and when they sat down Janet noticed something from the corner of her eye.

"Lily!" Janet whispered.

Lily didn't hear Janet, she was too focused on the reverend's speech.

She whispered a little louder, "LILY!"

"Not now, Janet!"

The reverend wrapped up and said a prayer. Lily walked up to where he was standing and said her speech.

"My father was a great man and he did a lot in his life. He was a wonderful father and a good husband to my mother. Josh Davis was very hard-working. He worked until the company had to push him out the door." People laughed and shed tears at the same time.

"He cared about everyone he met. I wish I could've spoken to him one last time. What I would give to hear another piece of advice, or to listen to another one of his silly jokes. So, Father, we'll all miss you dearly, and there won't be a day where I don't miss your goofy smile and laugh. Rest easy."

She pulled a tissue out of her pocket and wiped the tears away. She closed her eyes and tried not to think about anything, or she would shed a river of tears. In her heart she knew her father was with her mother again, and that thought brought peace to her. When Lily was looking at the crowd she paused and saw the three men from the coffee shop. She walked to the front row, and sat beside Janet.

"Janet the guys from the coffee shop are here!"

"That's what I was trying to tell you before you went up there."

"Oh, yeah, sorry I was rude. How did they know about the funeral?"

"I don't know. Maybe they knew your father and are paying their respect."

"Yeah, you're funny Janet, did you forget they tried to kill us last night? Twice. Whoever they are, they're not a friend to us."

"Well, we don't know for sure if it was them, but maybe if the Mercedes is parked here we would definitely know if it was them."

The reverend was done talking and everyone stood up from their seats. Janet and Lily slipped past people and sped back to the parking lot to see if they saw the Mercedes from the day before. They looked around and checked each car, but there was no black Mercedes to be found.

"Dang, I thought it would be here."

"Maybe they switched cars."

"Let's go back and wait until it's over, then we can see what car they go into."

"Good idea, Lily."

 They walked back to the burial area in a big field full of wildflowers. Everybody walked through a very long path, and it was time to bury Lily's father with her mother. Janet had her eyes fixed on the three men in the back of the standing crowd, but did not make it noticeable that she was watching them. The reverend said another prayer and everybody sang Wind Beneath My Wings before ending the ceremony.

 Lily was given a shovel and scooped some dirt to pour on the casket in the ground. The ceremony was over and everyone talked to Lily before they walked back to their cars. Lily and Janet were the last ones standing by Lily's father's grave. Lily started crying. Her face turned red like a fresh ripe apple at the end of summer. Her eyes started to get puffy from crying all day, she would have made a pond with all the tears she cried out. Janet gave Lily a hug and Janet walked Lily away from her father's grave.

They walked back to the parking lot to see what vehicle the three men went into. Janet spotted the men heading toward the middle of the parking lot and moved closer.

"Hey, there they are."

Lily wiped her tears away with a handkerchief and looked to where Janet was pointing.

"Yeah, I see them, they're going into that Silver BMW," Janet whispered.

"So, it's either they have two different cars or we are blaming the wrong people. Should we follow them?"

"No, let's look for the fourth clue while we're here."

They waited until the men driving the BMW were gone and started heading up the small hill where the ceremony was held.

"Where should we start Lily?"

"Well, the clue said something about the cemetery and it said below her name."

"So, let's look for something suspicious on a woman's stone."

They looked at the benches around the cemetery and searched some of the graves. An hour passed and they hadn't found anything.

"Lily, have you found anything yet?"

"No, nothing. How about you?"

"No, I couldn't see anything that looked like another clue."

They took a break for a few minutes and sat down on the nearest bench for a moment to think.

"Let's go over by my parent's graves. We didn't really check that area well."

They stood back up and walked on the path where Lily's parents were buried by. When Lily found her parents, she knelt down and looked at her father's gravestone. Lily then examined everything around both their graves, but didn't see anything. She then stared at her father's grave, still not wanting to believe he was really gone. Janet knelt right next to Lily to give her a hug, and talked about how he was able to see her mother in heaven and how they would both be together looking down at her.

Janet looked over at Lily's mother's grave and saw a flower vase with old crusty brown flowers. She grabbed the vase, tossed the flowers out, and went to get new ones in the field.

The air was filled with the sweet scent of blooming flowers, like a fragrant symphony. The sunlight kissed each flower petal, casting a warm glow over the field. There was such a vast amount of vibrant colors, as far as the eye could see. Janet had a hard time finding what flowers to pick, they all were so beautiful. Lily sat up against a big willow tree next to her parent's graves and looked out at the view of the field.

Janet walked back, put the flowers in the vase, and set it right next to Lily's mother's headstone. As she was putting the vase back, she read what was engraved on Lily's mother's headstone.

Amber G Davis

August 23, 1946 - June 14, 1989

Mother - Friend - Wife

<u>Ready For Love</u> - <u>Bad Company *</u>

Janet noticed something interesting and immediately shouted at Lily.

"Hey, I see a star like the ones on the paper!"

Lily walked over and looked at the bottom words of the headstone where Lily was pointing.

"Janet you found it!"

"That's a song, isn't it?"

"Yeah, my parents said they danced to this song at their wedding."

"This isn't much to go off of. Do you have any idea what this means?"

"I'm not sure, but it has the same star. That has to be it."

Janet took out a notepad and a pen from her purse to write down the clue so they didn't forget it.

"Well, now that we found the next clue, how about we go and eat some seafood from George's place," Lily suggested.

"That sounds great. I love seafood! But, on one condition."

"What's that?"

"I'm paying this time."

Lily giggled and went along with it.

"Ok, sounds fair."

They both stood up and Lily looked at her parent's graves wishing them goodbye. She took a moment to say a quick prayer and walked back to the car. Lily grabbed the car keys from her purse and unlocked the doors. Lily pulled out of the parking lot and drove down the road back to town with a little music to listen to. When they drove up to the stop sign by Harrison's barber shop, Lily turned left and drove towards the restaurant.

When Lily turned down another street she saw construction and had to wait for other cars to go on the other side before continuing.

"Seriously, construction? I'm getting so hungry," Janet said disappointed.

"Yeah, I am too. I can't stop thinking about seafood. I can already smell the crab. It was really good the last time I ate there and I'm excited for you to try it. His restaurant is one of a kind."

"Well, I hope we can eat it sometime today. This is taking forever."

"I don't know why it's taking this long."

Lily looked to her right and decided to take the side road.

"I'm going to take another road. This will be easier."

Lily turned out of the small line of cars and drove down a back road.

They turned down Jump Street and drove for a second before hitting a huge pothole. Lily and Janet bounced out of their seats and made their stomachs feel funny.

"Wow, is that why it's called Jump Street?"

   Janet and Lily looked at each other and laughed, before entering the George's Seafood restaurant.

Lily licked her lips. "Here we are."

"Yes, crab legs and grilled shrimp here I come."

Chapter X

Chocolate Supersize

   Lily and Janet stepped out of the car and waited for Janet to put on her jacket before going inside. A young couple came out of the restaurant and the young man held it open for Janet and Lily.

"Thank you, sir."

"No problem, you ladies have a nice evening"

   When they walked in the hostess assumed it was a table of two, but asked anyways if they were expecting anyone else. Janet said table of two and followed the woman after she grabbed their menus and two silverware bundles.

"Ok, follow me."

Lily and Janet followed the woman to their table and took a seat in a booth. Janet looked around the restaurant and saw a swordfish hanging from the ceiling and fish nets on the ocean-blue walls.

"Your waiter will be here shortly."

"Thank you," said Lily.

The woman placed the menus on the table and walked back to the front desk.

"Yes, we got another booth! I love booths, they are so much more comfortable!"

Janet bounced up and down on the squishy orange cushion as the waiter came around the corner.

"What would you both like to drink?"

"I'll have a pink lemonade," Lily responded back.

"And I'll just take some water," Janet said.

"Ok and do you know what you want to order?"

"No, not just yet."

"Ok, I'll be back with your drinks in a few minutes."

Janet took her notepad out of her purse and slid it over to Lily.

"So, have you thought about any ideas?" Asked Janet.

"No, all I know is that my parents danced to it at their wedding and it was my mom's favorite song."

"So, we have no leads so far."

"Yeah, we'll just have to look around and see if anything connects."

   Lily and Janet opened their menus and read the delicious food options. "The lobster looks so good," Lily said.

"Yes, it looks good. I think I'm going to get the crab and a salad."

   The waiter came back with their drinks, set them on the table, and gave them straws from his apron pocket. Then he put the tray under his arm and pulled out his small pad of paper and a pen to take their order.

"Do you know what you're going to order?"

"Yeah, I think we're ready, I'll have the lobster with a side of mashed potatoes and I'll take the shrimp appetizer as well," Lily said with a smile.

"Okay, and you miss?"

"I'll have the shrimp appetizer too, and I'll take the crab meal with the tossed house salad."

"Ok. I'll get these to George and I'll come back with those appetizers in a few minutes."

He came back with the appetizers and refilled their drinks. The shrimp was just right and their homemade sauce was fantastic. The food came twenty minutes later and the waiter put the warm plates on the table. "Those appetizers were good but this crab looks amazing!"

The waiter left and they both opened their napkins to get their silverware out. Lily dug into her food and almost half was gone in just a couple of minutes. Janet was about to eat her crab when she felt her plate.

"Ouch, this plate has some serious heat to it!"

Janet was stuck watching Lily eat her red lobster while she waited for hers to cool down.

"Mmmm, this is so good."

"Ok, you don't have to rub it in my face."

Lily laughed and continued eating. Janet blew on the crab and was finally able to tear into her food.

"Man, this is so good, it melts in my mouth. You were right about this place."

"Yeah, the crab is hard to beat, but when I ordered the lobster last time I remembered it was fantastic."

Janet took another bite of the delicious crab and her eyes got as big as golf balls.

"Dang, I can't get over this dish, we need to come here again."

Janet and Lily were already stuffed from their meal and realized they both needed boxes. If they had another bite, they would burst. Janet asked for boxes and while they waited Janet went up to the front desk to pay for both meals.

Janet left the table and, not so long after, an older man in his thirties came out of the kitchen with a piece of chocolate cake and a small grin on his face. His hair was dark brown and he was wearing a George's seafood t-shirt with blue jeans. He walked up to Lily's table and set the cake down in front of her. Lily looked at him with confusion, and didn't know how to react.

"The chef told me to pick someone for a free dessert tonight."

His voice was deep, and Lily thought it was out of the ordinary, but she accepted the kind gesture.

"Fantastic," the man said.

He walked back to the kitchen and Lily started to lick the frosting off her fork. Janet sat back down after paying the bill and gave Lily a 'what the heck look'.

"Where did that come from?" Janet asked.

"A waiter gave it to me saying it was for free!"

"That's kinda odd."

"Yeah, but it looked so good I couldn't resist, even though I'm stuffed." Lily took a bite and slid back into her seat, she had forgotten how delicious and rich the cake was. She went for another bite, but when she put her fork in the cake it hit something hard, something that wasn't supposed to be in there. Lily looked up at Janet and both their eyes got wider. Lily quickly grabbed another fork, pried open the cake, and couldn't believe what she saw.

"Oh my god, Lily! Is that what I think it is?"

She looked at numbers counting down. 22, 21, 20, 19.

"IT'S A BOMB!"

Lily sat up immediately and shouted at everyone to get out of the building.

"EVERYBODY OUT! THERE'S A BOMB!" There wasn't much time. 11, 10, 9, 8…. Lily told Janet to go with everyone and Lily ran as fast as she could towards the back exit. She opened the door and threw the bomb as far as she could outside, running away in the opposite direction down the street.

Lily ran down the alleyway towards the main street and had only a few seconds to get to safety when the bomb went off. BOOM! She was pushed by the explosion of the bomb and fell hard onto the ground. She looked back and watched the fire consume the restaurant. Lily turned her head back slowly and looked forward. Her vision was slightly blurry and only could make out bigger objects. Lily couldn't ignore the pain from the ringing in both ears. Her right arm had small pebbles pressed into her large bloody scrape, from the fall.

She slowly moved her left hand and wiped off some of the pebbles. Lily looked up again and saw a man a couple of feet away on the sidewalk. The man was the waiter who gave her the cake, he stared at Lily and then did something unexpected. He started to pull off his beard. She then recognized who he was, the man had one misty gray eye and one yellowish-green. The black Mercedes pulled up and he jumped in.

The Mercedes drove off fast and Lily could slightly hear an ambulance, fire trucks, and cop cars coming towards the restaurant. She saw the bright lights stop on the street and a few men running toward her. That was the last thing she saw before passing out.

One man lifted Lily's head and realized she was out. They lifted Lily and put her on a stretcher.

When they were carrying Lily back to the ambulance the fireman started to put out the fire that was rising higher and higher. Janet jogged to the ambulance and saw Lily being carried on a stretcher. She told the men lifting her that she was with Lily, and quickly jumped into the back of the ambulance to ride with Lily to the hospital.

When they arrive at the hospital they put Lily in room 112. The doctor came out and let Janet in the room after they examined her. She walked in and saw Lily sleeping on the bed, Janet saw a chair and pulled it closer to the bed to watch over Lily until she woke.

Two hours passed. Janet was taking a nap in the chair snoozing away while she waited for Lily to wake up. Janet's snoring woke Lily up. She looked around the room and realized she was at the hospital.

"Janet. Janet, wake up."

Janet blinked sleepily and stretched.

"Hey, how are you feeling?"

"I'm kind of sore everywhere. Did I pass out?"

"Yep, after everyone ran out people called the police. They found you passed out on the ground near where the bomb exploded, then they took you to the hospital."

"How long was I out?"

"About two hours. It's around five right now."

"Lily, Sergeant Jackson and Officer Cannon are outside the door waiting to question you, they already questioned me while you were sleeping."

"I was thinking, should we tell them about the clues, and who we think it is?"

"Yeah, I think we should, I'll tell the sergeant. Janet, after the explosion my vision went a little blurry, but I saw the man who gave me the piece of cake going into the Mercedes!"

"Oh my God, Lily, you were targeted! They tried to kill you. How could we have been so dumb? Your father told us not to trust anyone. We need to be more careful, that's the third time."

The doctor and the two police came into the room and walked around Lily's bed.

"How are you doing Miss. Davis?" Asked the doctor.

"I have a headache and my right arm aches."

"Yes, it's going to be sore for a few days, that was a nasty cut. I'm going to come back and check on you, then we'll see if you can leave."

"Thank you."

"I'll be right back."

The doctor walked out of the room, and Sergeant Jackson and Officer Cannon walked up closer to the bed.

"We need to ask you a few questions about the explosion."

Lily explained to them about the waiter giving her the cake and the bomb being inside it. She told them she didn't know about the bomb and she did what she thought was best to get rid of it. Lily mentioned the clues and the Mercedes, and described what the man looked like. The sergeant was shocked about what Lily had just told them, but he had never seen this man before. He told the girls to call for help if anything happened again and to be more careful from now on.

"We'll send out some officers tomorrow to search for the Mercedes and find the people you described to me."

Sergeant Jackson asked for a moment to talk to Lily alone. He waited for Janet to close the door and pulled up a chair next to Lily.

"What have you both walked into?"

"Honestly Sergeant, I have no idea why this is happening to us, and right after my father died. It couldn't be a worse time."

"I moved here from a big city and I've seen some horrific things I wish I hadn't seen. With the information you just told me, you are being targeted for either something you did or because they want something from you."

"They want my father's gold."

"What?" The Sergeant said confused.

"We received that call this morning before those gunshots and they said they wanted the gold. My father must've struck gold when he worked in the mines. They must think I have it."

"This is pretty serious, Lily. Whoever wants that gold, they'll do anything to get it in their hands."

There was a moment of silence. Lily didn't know what to think. She looked back at the sergeant and asked if he and Officer Cannon would keep watch near the house until they could find what her father left for her. He told her they would watch a block away and if they needed them he would be there. She felt some relief knowing her block would be watched.

The Sergeant put his hat on, walked out of the room, and left the hospital with his partner. When they finished, Janet and the doctor both came into the room. The doctor examined Lily one last time and told her she could leave. The doctor told her she would be sore for a few days but nothing too serious. He gave her some forms to fill out and told her to wait for the nurse to grab it before they left. Lily slowly stood up, stretched, and grabbed her coat that was hanging on the coat rack. Janet grabbed both their purses and they walked out of room 112.

When Janet and Lily arrived at the front desk, Lily gave the woman the signed papers and they walked out of the hospital. Lily squinted her eyes trying to avoid the blinding sun when walking to the car. Janet opened the door for her and Lily slid in the passenger seat.

"Janet, should we stop at the store and grab a few things to eat before we head to the house?"

"Yeah, probably. The fridge is about empty. Where is it at?"

"It's on Twin Elm Street, by Casey's ice cream shop."

"Oh, I know where that is, we passed It yesterday."

Janet drove out of the parking lot and stopped at the store. She went in and grabbed a few groceries, while Lily took a nap in the car. Lily helped put the groceries in the back and offered to drive home.

Janet rolled down the window and stuck her head out like a dog on the way home. Feeling the wind hitting her face felt so free. She tried to search for the big dipper in the dark sky, but realized that it was probably behind her since she couldn't find it anywhere in sight. When they arrived back at the house, Lily pulled into the driveway and found a surprise waiting for them. Their headlights shined on the house revealing the open front door and a black Mercedes in the driveway.

Chapter XI

Break-In

"Oh my god, Lily! The house was broken into."

"I see that. well, let's call the cops again."

"Uh, yeah, cause we don't know if someone is still in there. Heck, I'm not going in until it's checked out."

"We can wait in the car until they get here," Lily said as she locked the car doors.

Lily backed out of the driveway and pulled up next to the mailbox. Janet called the police while Lily was watching the house like a hawk, seeing if anyone came out. Sergeant Jackson answered and was very concerned when Janet quickly explained what they saw when they pulled into the driveway.

He told Janet that he and Officer Cannon would come back and investigate then hung up the phone.

"Sergeant Jackson answered and said he and Officer Cannonwould come over here as fast as they could."

"I bet they're so tired of getting calls from us. I mean, three calls in two days," Lily said laughing.

"Yeah, probably, they might as well spend the night with us."

They waited in the car for a minute or two, watching the house and watching for when the cops would pull up. They arrived two minutes after they called and pulled up next to Lily's father's car to talk to the two girls.

"We're going to check in the house, if it's safe Sergeant Jackson will come out and tell you it's clear."

They both opened their car doors and stepped out. Sergeant Jackson took out his gun, held it down by his side with both hands and started jogging towards the house with caution. Officer Cannon followed and when they approached the front door they both stopped and whipped out their guns pointing them inside the house.

Sargent Jackson went in first and Officer Cannon followed. They were gone for a good five minutes searching rooms and every nook and cranny. Lily and Janet were waiting and waiting for them to come back out. Lily looked up and spotted something in her bedroom window. It was a man wearing all-black clothing and a gray face mask. Right when Lily saw him, he disappeared from the window.

"Janet, there is someone in my room! We have to tell Sergeant Jackson."

"NO, LILY! That's too dangerous, they said they would check it out. They'll get him."

After Janet finished her sentence, there was a loud gunshot.

"Did that come from the house?" Janet asked.

"No, it came from the bushes. Yes it came from the house, you goof," Lily said sarcastically.

"I hope Officer Cannon and Sergeant Jackson didn't get shot."

They stared at the house and everything was silent. The girls were waiting for action, for someone to come out of the house, but nothing. Janet didn't know what to think. They had no idea what had happened or who shot their gun. Then they saw Sergeant Jackson coming out the front door carrying his partner in his arms. Lily and Janet ran over to Sergeant Jackson and immediately saw what was wrong with Officer Cannon. She had been shot on the right side above her hip.

She was losing blood quickly and needed to get to the hospital immediately. He had great strength carrying her to the car. He opened the car door, laid her down on the back seat, and took his vest off because it was soaked in her blood. He pulled out his tucked shirt, ripped a piece off the bottom, and gave it to Janet to press on her wound.

Sergeant Jackson jogged up front to the driver's seat and grabbed his walkie-talkie to call for backup. Lily and Janet comforted Officer Cannon, hoping to distract her mind. Lily looked up and saw three men run out of the kitchen door. They ran quickly to the Mercedes, before Sergeant Jackson noticed them, and started their car. Sergeant Jackson could hear the car starting. He quickly rushed out of the front seat and ran towards the moving Mercedes. Sergeant Jackson held his gun up to the car and yelled, "Stop the vehicle!"

The driver didn't stop, the car kept moving backward and then onto the road. Sergeant Jackson shot his gun at the vehicle but the car swerved making black marks, and drove off into town. Sergeant Jackson didn't bother running after knowing they would be gone in no time.

He ran back to his car and wrote something down. Lily sprinted over to Sergeant Jackson, disappointed that the Mercedes got away.

"Dammit, they got away."

"Yes, but I saw their license plate and when I get back at the station I'll track them down."

"Thank you so much. We need to find these guys so they don't hurt anyone else," Lily remarked.

"Don't worry, we will do the best we can. When we leave, make sure to lock all your doors, and it would be best if you stayed near each other tonight."

"We'll do that. It's all because of me this is happening."

"What do you mean?" He questioned.

"Ever since we arrived things have been happening to us. We've been threatened multiple times and I was almost killed. I feel like there is a deeper meaning than them just wanting my father's gold."

"I don't know what they want, but we will keep you and Janet safe.

"Thank you, I feel a lot safer when you are around."

 He turned away and walked towards the car. Lily could tell he was hiding a smile from her. In the front of the car, Sergeant Jackson turned around and looked behind his seat to check on Officer Cannon, who was gripping Janet's hand to relieve her pain.

"How's my partner doing?"

"I'm hanging in there, just wish the bullet was out."

Lily could hear the ambulance getting closer. Two came down the street, with their red and blue lights brightening up the neighborhood and their sirens deafening to the ear. The block was so colorful and bright that Lily felt like it was Christmas.

The ambulance and police pulled up next to Lily's car and two paramedics rushed out. They rushed over to Officer Cannon and helped her out of the car seat and put her on a stretcher. She groaned from the pain and gripped the side of the stretcher as they put her into the ambulance. Before they sped off, Janet told her she would be alright and that she would visit her in the hospital. Sergeant Jackson and Lily watched cops flood into her father's house, checking for anything that could help them identify the men.

"We'll find these guys trust us."

He grabbed her hand and gave her a paper with a phone number.

"If you need anything, call me. I won't let them hurt you or Janet."

He looked into Lily's eyes and she could tell, then, he was sweet on her. He smiled and assured her it was safe after the cop's search was over. Then he took off and followed the other cop cars to the station.

Lily and Janet were now alone. The block wasn't so bright any longer. The streetlights cast long shadows, creating an eerie atmosphere. There was almost a complete blanket of darkness and that made Lily feel even more unsteady. Lily quickly jumped in the car and parked it in the garage. Janet made sure to lock all the doors in the house and to check all the windows. They both checked downstairs to see if anything was taken or missing, but it was hard to tell if something was gone. The house was a labyrinth of books off the shelves and all over the floor, boxes in the family room were dumped, and every cabinet was checked and opened.

"Those men made a mess down here. I wonder what the upstairs looks like."

  Lily followed Janet, racing up the stairs to check their rooms. Janet stepped into her room and saw her bed unmade, the nightstand drawers open, and her suitcase lying open on the ground cluttered with clothes on top. It was a mess. She checked for anything missing and found the only thing taken was her grandma's antique silver earrings. From across the room, she saw a note taped on the mirror and walked over to see what it said. Janet picked it up and read the blue ink on the small paper.

I will get that gold Miss. Davis

You better watch your back. I'm coming for you.

X DS

Her eyes widened after reading the threat on the paper in her hands. She folded it and walked across the hall to Lily's room to see how bad her room looked.

Lily was walking around her room picking up things on the floor. Her room was worse than Janet's, it took her a minute to realize the gold tree key that was lying on one of the nightstands is missing. She turned around and saw Janet standing in the doorway with a worried look.

"Janet, they took the key! What if we need it for another clue?"

"Seriously, man, we should've taken it with us. They took my grandmother's antique silver earrings, too. I can never replace those."

"Oh, I'm so sorry, Janet! Those dirty little --!"

Lily looked down at the small note in Janet's hand.

"What's that?"

"Oh yeah, one of the men left this on my mirror!"

Janet handed the note to Lily and she read the threat from one of the robbers.

"I'm coming for you, that line is so cliche, but seriously we should give this to Sergeant Jackson tomorrow. It might have fingerprints on it, and these Initials look so similar.

"I noticed that. We need to remember those initials. Maybe we can find his name, I wonder if he knew your father sometime in the past."

"Well, let's go downstairs to get those groceries in the house so we can finally eat. I'm surprisingly hungry. After eating so much earlier you would think I wouldn't be," said Janet.

"Yeah, for some reason I'm kind of hungry myself."

Lily put the note on her nightstand and they both walked down the stairs to put away the groceries that they left in the car. After the groceries were put away Lily returned to the back door and locked it.

"You want to have sandwiches and potato chips, Lily?"

"Yeah. Oh, and pickles, I love pickles!"

Janet set the plates on the table along with the chips, bread, colby cheese, and turkey lunch meat. Lily opened one of the only cabinets that wasn't already opened from the break-in and grabbed some napkins.

"You won't believe what happened before the cops left," said Lily smiling.

"What happened?"

"Well, Sergeant Jackson gave me his personal number. Then, he looked me in the eyes and I could see something different in him. I think he likes me."

"Oh, Lily, that's so cute, maybe you guys can go out sometime this week!"

"Yeah, maybe, but I feel like I shouldn't lead him on since we're going back to California."

"You can always write to each other and if things work out he could move to California."

They ate their sandwiches, potato chips, and pickles and, after Janet finished, she sat up to put her plate in the sink while Lily was still eating pickles out of the jar.

"I think I'll go to bed early tonight. We had a long day, especially you Lily."

"Yeah, I think I'll go take a shower and go to bed, as well. I still have a small headache, so it might take me a minute to fall asleep."

The girls went upstairs, took showers, and settled in for the night. Lily had a hard time falling asleep. She tossed and turned and eventually made herself tired by walking around in circles. It was an hour or two after her head hit the pillow that her sleep was interrupted by a phone call. She sat up and rubbed her eyes, then checked the time on the clock. It was 10:35 pm. Lily answered the phone and heard a man's voice on the other side talking. It was Sergeant Jackson.

"Sorry this is a late call, but I wanted to tell you that I went back to the station and found out the license plate was stolen."

   Lily was bummed about the news and told Sergeant Jackson about the note Janet found in her room after everyone left.

"That's a good start. At least we know his initials. We can ask people around town if they know anyone with those initials!"

"Also, Officer Cannon is resting and the doctor said she'll be ok. She's going to have to stay three weeks in the hospital."

"That's good to hear! Janet and I will visit her tomorrow and bring her some flowers. I also wanted to give you the note to see if there are any possible fingerprints on it. You'll have to be careful touching it, our fingerprints are on it already."

"I was about to say the same thing. I'll be at the station from 10 am to 3 in the afternoon. And, I'm glad you're coming to the station because I need to give you and Janet something, something very important."

Lily was curious and excited about what Sergeant Jackson wanted to give to her and wondered why he sounded so serious about it.

"Ok, we will stop by tomorrow. Thank you for everything Sergeant, this has been stressful these last few days. Not to mention scary!"

"Please, call me Owen. And, don't worry, we'll find them soon and you'll be back in California in no time."

"Well, goodnight Owen, I'll see you tomorrow."

"Goodnight, Lily."

Lily was over the moon happy. She felt like a schoolgirl. Lily put the phone back on the nightstand and rolled over to get some sleep. She stared at the fan above her and watched it spin around and around. Lily was thinking about her parents and had a thought, she was no one's little girl anymore. But, knows her parents are watching over her and keeping her safe every day. Tears rolled down her face, one after another, and soaked the side of her pillow. She pulled her hoodie sleeve over her hand and wiped her wet face. Lily sniffed and cleared her throat then closed her eyes and started to dream, so she wouldn't have any more thoughts. She needed her rest for what was coming tomorrow.

Chapter XII

The Portrait

    The morning was vivid and cheerful, with a cool soft breeze, birds chirping on the electric lines, and the grass wet from the rain. She decides to get up. Blinded by the sun shining on her face, Lily's drapes were half open, enough for the sun to shine through the window.

    Lily opens her drapes fully to look outside. She sees her old neighbor walking up towards his mailbox in only his underwear and wool robe. She looks away, eyes burning from what she saw. Lily goes to her closet where her clothes are hanging and picks a pair of black leggings, a blue and white flannel, and slips on her Sperry white sneakers. She pulled her hair back in a high ponytail and then walked back over to the bed to put on her tennis shoes. Putting on her shoes she smelled something coming from the kitchen that made her stomach rumble. It was the smell of blueberry muffins rising in the oven, and crispy bacon sizzling in the pan ready for Lily to devour them.

Lily comes out of her room running down the stairs eyeing the blueberry muffins Janet was taking out of the oven.

"Morning, did you sleep well?" asked Janet.

"Morning! Yeah, I slept great. My headache went away, but the doctor was right, I'm still sore. By the way, those muffins smell delicious! How did you make those? I don't remember seeing blueberries in the bags last night?"

"I went out early this morning and bought them. Blueberry muffins sounded good to me, so I woke up craving them."

"Well, thanks, I must've been deep asleep to not hear you go out."

Lily walked over to the counter where the muffins were sitting. She grabbed two plates from the cupboard and gave one of them to Janet, showing that she wanted to eat them right away, even if they were steaming hot.

She grabbed a knife, loosening the muffins from inside the pan, and grabbed two to start with. One of them being the biggest muffin. Lily grabbed a couple of bacon strips from the pan on the stove and opened the fridge to get the butter and milk. She looked around in the fridge searching for them, but neither the butter or milk was in there.

"Oh, I've got the butter and the milk already on the table. I knew you would want to crack into these muffins and didn't want to waste precious time," Janet laughed.

"Thanks, I can't wait to eat these! My stomach is going nuts."

Lily sat down with her plate and started eating the delicious breakfast Janet made for them. Lily sliced her muffins down the middle, letting the steam escape. She then pulls open the butter lid and scrapes some butter onto her knife and spreads it on all the muffin pieces over and over again. She bit into one of the steaming muffin pieces. She then licked her lips, picking up a blueberry that fell on her lip. The butter melted in her mouth and the blueberries were so juicy and ripe. It went so well with the milk that cooled down her throat.

"This is the best muffin I've ever tasted! How did you make these?"

"It's my mom's recipe. I've memorized it so well because we made them every Sunday when I was a kid. I can give you the recipe, it has only a few ingredients."

Lily shoved another muffin chunk into her mouth. "Yes please! They're amazing!"

"Hey Lily, I heard the phone ring last night in your room. Was it those men calling again?"

"No, it was Owen calling about the license plate on the car."

"Oh, did they find who it was?"

"No, he said it was stolen but he's made sure cops parked around town today to watch out for the Mercedes. He also said that Officer Cannon was doing well and she would be in the hospital for a few weeks."

"Well, that's good that she's feeling better. I thought we could go souvenir shopping in town since this is my first time in Maine, and maybe we can go pick some flowers out at the flower shop to give to Officer Cannon."

"That sounds fun. I love shopping and I think Officer Cannon will like a visit. Hospitals can get lonely. Shopping will get our minds off of everything that happened these past few days."

Janet finished up the bacon that she was holding in her hand and drank the rest of her orange juice. Lily decided to wash the dishes since Janet made breakfast, while Janet did her hair and cleaned up. Janet started walking up the stairs heading towards her room to change her shirt that had flour all over it and changed her hair into a low messy bun. While she was putting her right earring, she yelled down at Lily to ask for some perfume. "Hey Lily, can I use a squirt of perfume?"

"Yeah, go ahead."

"Is it in the bathroom?"

"No, I think it's on my dresser."

"Ok, thanks."

   Janet went across the hall to Lily's room and found the perfume sitting on her dresser just as Lily had said. Janet looked up and waved the vanilla and coconut perfume around her, spraying it all over her body. As she put the perfume back down on the dresser she noticed something that looked familiar, something she knew she had heard of before.

   She stared at it for a few seconds, those few seconds turned into minutes and then she knew where she had heard it before.

"Lily get up here. I think you'll want to look at this!" Janet shouted.

"Ok, let me wash this last plate."

   Lily rushed the washing and rinsing, leaving a mess of bubbles on the plate when she placed it on the drying rack. Lily pulled her gloves off and ran up the stairs as fast as she could.

"What is it?" Lily asked in suspense.

   Janet walked over to the dresser to see if Lily could spot what she had seen.

"Do you see it?"

"What? My perfume?"

"No Lily, look a little to your left."

Lily's eyes looked down at the floor next to the dresser.

"The box of old picture albums?" Lily asked.

"No, try looking up at the wall above that."

Lily looked up and looked at the old painting hanging next to her dresser. "Is it the painting?" asked Lily, still confused.

"Yes, but look a little harder."

Lily examined every inch of it then she realized why Janet was so excited. The painting had writing on the bottom of the painting of the song that was engraved on her mother's grave. Excitement ran through Lily when she realized that was the next clue. It was in her room the whole time.

"Finally, I thought you would never see it," Janet chuckled.

"How did we not realize that this was it? I must've passed it a thousand times. It was never mine, my father must've put it in my room when he made these clues."

"I wonder what the clue is. It has to be on it," remarked Janet.

"Or behind it."

They both stared at the painting seeing if they could find what it was they were looking for. The next clue: possibly a note, another key, or code to punch into something. The painting was the album of the song, it was the most creative piece of art. Lily grabbed the sides of the painting and lifted it off the wall. She turned it around and saw nothing but cardboard and a hook for hanging the painting. They were confused and didn't understand where the next clue was on the painting. Then it hit Lily, she bent down and laid the painting face down.

She opened the backside revealing a piece of paper taped down, it was the fifth clue. She pulled it slowly, trying not to rip the paper stuck to it. Once it was off Lily handed it to Janet for her to read it out loud while she put the painting back together and on the wall like it was once before. "What does it say," Lily asked.

"It says:

'More than once you checked me out, took me home, and read out loud. I was your favorite when you were five, find me now don't worry you have time. *' "

Lily thought hard and asked herself, what does that mean?

"That's a hard one," Janet remarked.

"Yeah, I just have to think what I liked when I was five, but I don't remember that far."

The words re-ran in Lily's head over, over, and over as she read the paper. She thought about all her childhood memories, many flashed back to her. She could see her playing with her old friends, her mom pushing her on the swings at the park, and her seventh birthday party when her dad's best friend dressed as a clown had scared her to death and she kicked his shin with her foot.

Lily could remember the good times when it was raining and they camped in the living room, cooking chicken soup on the stove instead of hot dogs over the fire. Or the many times they went fishing and caught nothing so they went to the grocery store to buy fish, and ended up buying ice cream down the road too.

She remembered the bad times that she wished weren't there still, like when she tried to help put away dishes one summer and broke a couple of plates in the process. Her mom berated her for breaking them and she had to go to her room for the night. And the time Lily was around six when she saw her dad's friend flip someone off, thinking it meant being friendly or another way to say hello. A few days later when she met her first-grade teacher she gave the same sign to her and her teacher was, as Lily remembered, appalled by what her first-grader did. Lily remembered going to the office that morning and talking to the principal about her actions and explaining that she thought it meant to be nice.

Lily laughed looking back at her childhood moments but couldn't think of anything that matched the clue. She turned to Janet for any ideas she had of what the paper meant.

"It says more than once you checked me out, maybe a movie or perhaps something from school?" Lily said to herself.

"Well, it says you took me home to read out loud, so it couldn't be a movie." Janet looked at Lily quickly, "How about a book?"

"Yes, that's it, I GOT IT! When I was five I loved this series called 'Julie Of The Wolves'. I used to get them from the library in town and checked them out all the time. My mom used to read a chapter or two to me at night."

"So, we have to go to the town library next I'm guessing," remarked Janet.

"Yep, that's our next destination. We can do that later today after we shop and stop to talk to Owen and Officer Cannon."

"This will be a productive day. I can't wait to find some cool souvenirs to take home with me."

"Me too, I have a few in mind and I'll save the best one for last. It has everything you could think of," Lily said excitedly.

Lily and Janet grabbed the clues just in case of another break-in and grabbed the note that the men left in Janet's room. While Janet finished getting ready Lily went downstairs to pack a lunch for them to eat after doing a little shopping. Janet comes down with both their purses and sets Lily's purse on the table near the counter. She opens her purse and shoves the notes in so they don't lose them, along with her small notepad. She looks over and sees Lily packing cut ham and cheese sandwiches, pickles, and some fruit in a lunch bag.

"Are you packing us a lunch for later?"

"Yeah, I thought instead of going out to eat we could just eat in the car or go to the lake."

"That sounds nice. No bombs, no unknown enemies, just peace."

Lily laughed and finished putting the washed fruit in a container. She put everything in a medium-sized red lunch box and put some ice in to keep everything cold.

"Janet, are you ready to go have fun?"

"Are you kidding? I've been ready all morning!"

Janet grabbed their purses, the lunch box and opened the door to the garage. They put their stuff in the back of the car. Lily pulled out of the driveway and started to drive down the street. They drove into town and passed George's Seafood. The restaurant was closed off with yellow police tape, wrapping around the building like a big Christmas present. The parking lot was empty with glass all over the sidewalk from the broken windows.

"Wow, look at the place. It looks terrible. I hope they get it fixed up quickly," said Janet.

"Yeah, that bomb did some damage. That's too bad, it's such a good restaurant."

Lily pulled into a big parking lot, there were only a few cars so it was easy to find a parking spot. There were three shops for souvenirs, one of the buildings being bigger with an upstairs.

Once they were parked Lily and Janet grabbed their purses and locked the car doors. The girls walked up to the smaller shop first. It was a cute old shop with some white, blue, and purple flowers in the front. In the window, there were three mannequins with t-shirts and hoodies on them showing off the variety of clothing they sell. There were also bracelets and mugs in the window, the shop looked very interesting. They opened the front door and walked into an antique and souvenir shop.

A woman who looked like she was sixty said hello to Lily and Janet when they walked in. The store was a labyrinth of clothes racks everywhere and collector items on every shelf around the store. There was a whole aisle dedicated to different types of mugs and, on another aisle there were picture frames, jewelry, paintings, and anything you could think of. Janet and Lily split up looking for something cool they could buy. Janet found a rack with a huge variety of postcards and looked around to see which one she liked the best. She picked one up that had the state of Maine printed on it and that said Harpswell on the front. Janet looked around some more and found a crab pepper and salt shaker.

"That would look so neat on the table."

Lily came around the corner with a Maine shirt and a pair of bear slippers. "I see you found some things," she said.

"Yeah, I found this cool salt and pepper shaker. I love it, it will look cool in my kitchen back home. I like those slippers. They look so comfortable."

Janet reached out and felt the slippers Lily was going to buy. They were so fuzzy and soft that she had to get herself a pair. They walked to the front desk by the door and waited in line behind an angry man. The man was very adamant about the price he wanted for the ring he picked out in the display case. After a few minutes of yelling and demanding a lower price for the ring, the old lady gave him the lowest price she could offer and he took it. He paid and stormed out of the shop and the old woman had a sigh of relief that he was out of her store.

"Sorry about that ladies, some people can be just straight-up rude and very un-adult-like."

The old woman started to check out Lily's items first.

"That's alright, we're in no hurry and he was quite rude. He shouldn't talk to anyone like that. We're just having a souvenir shopping day."

"That's always fun on vacation, where are you girls from?"

"I grew up here but we live in California."

"Oh, that is a beautiful state! I visited California when I was in my forties. My favorite state is Tennessee, if you haven't been there you should visit. My husband and I were on our second honeymoon there when we went hiking and we found a small cave. He was curious back then, always wanting to see and explore new things. I was curious too but the cave didn't look that safe. The rocks were caving in from the sides and it looked like no one had been in there in a long time.

Her eyes widened recounting the story.

There was a dirty sign beside the entry that said 'Do Not Enter Danger,' so I told him we should move on, but he didn't listen. He went into the cave and when he went in I watched carefully for any bad signs. He yelled from inside and said he found a small piece of gold. I told him to come out of the cave because it made me very nervous. He came out and when my husband showed me that piece of gold my eyes lit up, it was the size of your thumb nail! A real small gold nugget. It was an incredible trip. I'll never forget it."

"Wow, that sounds like it was a good vacation, maybe we'll have to go hiking there!" Lily chuckled.

The old woman was done checking them out and Janet put money in a tip jar she had on the counter.

"Thank you ladies. You have a wonderful trip here in Maine."

"Thank you Mrs."

"Oh please, all my friends call me Amanda!"

"Well Amanda, you have a great day," Lily replied.

The girls opened the door and walked out of the shop.

"Janet, you want to go to this one next?"

"Yeah, let's hit them all, I love shopping."

The shop next door was just as charming. The siding was a light blue and there were also flowers in pots by the front door. The smell of flowers was so strong and smelled amazing, like smelling a fresh cake coming out of the oven but floral. When they walked in it was a bigger shop than the one before, the walls had trees and rivers painted on them with birds flying in the sky. An eagle with a trout in its mouth was painted by the front door flying away from a lake.

The shop had similar items from the previous store. There were racks of t-shirts, hoodies, and different types of slippers. In the middle there was a shelf for mugs and decorative plates. Lily went to the hoodie section and found a medium hoodie with Harpswell written on the front. She couldn't pass up the price, fifty percent off, so she had to buy it. Lily looked over and saw Janet with a plant in her hand and what looked like a key chain. Lily went to look at the mugs and was amazed.

"Their selection is larger!"

There were cups with animal prints, cups that looked like food, there was one that was a bear face. But the one that caught her eye was the one that looked like a fish head. Lily grabbed the coffee mug and looked around some more. She ended up finding a lobster charm for her bracelet and a book that looked interesting to read. Janet walked up to her with a handful of things: a plant, a green Maine shirt, a key chain, and a bag of hard candy.

"Hey, you found some good stuff."

"Yeah I like this mug, it looks like the one I had as a kid. I broke that one and I broke a mug before we went to Hawaii so I needed a replacement. I get a charm for every trip I take. I put it on my charm bracelet my father got me when we went to Mexico to see some ruins."

"Oh yeah, your charm bracelet, I remember when we took that trip to South Dakota you got that charm of Teddy Roosevelt's head."

"That was one of my favorite charms, and that was such a good trip."

"Are you done shopping?" Janet asked.

"Yeah, I found some good things here, let's checkout and hit the next one."

Lily couldn't wait to put her charm on her bracelet and read her book that night. They walked out with their bags from the first gift shop and the bags from the second gift shop.

"Do you want to put the bags in the car? I don't think I can carry and shop with both of these in my hands?"

"Yeah, I was thinking the same thing, mine are heavy," Lily replied.

They walked past the smaller shop and into the parking lot. Lily opened the back seat and they put their bags on the floor so Janet's hard candy didn't melt from the hot sun.

"Are you ready for the biggest store? You're going to like this one, it's cool," Lily stopped herself, so she would stop herself from spoiling the surprise inside.

"Well, you'll see when we get in. I've been here multiple times!"

"Now I really can't wait."

Lily and Janet walked across the parking lot and looked at the windows in the store. There was jewelry displayed, shirts, mugs, key chains, headbands, and toys. There were so many things in the window it drew your attention, making you want to walk straight into the store.

"Oh my! I think I'm going to get that purse, it looks gorgeous," Janet said.

She opened the door and her eyes lit up.

"Wow, look at this place, this is the nicest gift shop I've ever been to!"

Janet was standing in front of a giant cylinder fish tank going all the way up to the ceiling. It was the most beautiful fish tank of all different types of fish swimming around and around.

"That's probably very entertaining for the owners to watch every day. You would never get bored."

"Yeah, I think it's really neat! Very unique."

There were also paintings on the walls. A painting of a ship out at sea, and a lighthouse on a hill facing the ocean were some. A few kids were looking at a bin of toys, and one kid asked their mom if they could get a firetruck for being good. At the back of the building was a staircase leading to the upstairs. Janet went upstairs looking around for any more damage she could get into. As she went up she could immediately see the purse she liked from the window. She went to see what the price was and it was better than she expected.

Lily was doing her shopping downstairs, grabbing another hoodie that she fell in love with immediately. She picked up a green headband with leaves printed on it, and a pack of scented pens. Lily went over to the big candy section in the back right corner. She was craving some sweets and wanted something with caramel. When she picked up the salted caramel Lily looked below and saw the chocolate-covered almond packages from the plane. She walked around the store looking for Janet and ended up finding her in the bathroom.

"You won't believe what I found. Come with me!"

"Ok, let me wash my hands. What did you find?"

"I found the chocolate almonds we like."

"This day just got even better!"

Lily showed Janet where the chocolate almonds were and Janet grabbed nine long packages.

"I hope they don't have a limit on items, I'm going to take the whole shelf."

Lily laughed and grabbed two of the packages so she could have some too. "I'm done, do you want to check out?"

"Yeah, I think I'm done shopping for today."

Janet and Lily bought their items and Janet took one last look at the giant cylinder fish tank before they walked out of the store.

"That was fun. I need to check my account when we get back to your dad's house to see how much I spent today."

"I'm going to do the same thing. I didn't go crazy, but I like to spoil myself sometimes. Hey, you want to get flowers for Officer Cannon and visit, or go eat first?"

"Well, it is twelve thirty so eat first, then visit."

"Ok, perfect because I'm hungry too."

Lily started the car and drove to the park in town. When they finished eating their cheese and ham sandwiches they were on their way to the flower shop to get some flowers for Officer Cannon.

"What flowers do you want to get for her?"

"How about some daisies or roses, every girl loves roses."

"Yeah, we can get her a variety. Maybe some red, white, peach, or yellow. They have rows and rows of all types of flowers and you can make your own bouquet."

"That's neat. I don't know any shops that let you make your own bouquet."

"I know, she is a nice lady. I grew up picking flowers for her shop. I would go to the shoreline and pick wildflowers all afternoon. I put them all in my red wagon and when I got back she would pay me a few dollars for doing it. I liked doing it for her too. The shoreline was quiet and peaceful. It was nice to go out there and feel the wind blowing and to hear the waves hit the rocks."

"Sounds pleasant. I wish I grew up here, it's such a nice town."

"Look, we're here! I'm excited I haven't seen her in a few years."

Lily pulled into the parking lot and locked the doors. When the girls walked up to the shop they opened the door and walked in. Inside was just how Lily remembered, rows of different colorful flowers. There were shelves by the front window that had a dozen pots of flowers that you could hang from the porch. Janet walked to the back of the shop passing tons of flowers. She looked at the labels in front of all the flowers and picked up a few pink geraniums. Lily finds the lady at the front desk helping a customer. She heads over to the front desk and, when she's done helping her customers, she notices Lily approaching the desk.

"Lily, is that you?"

"Yep, it's me."

The woman whipped around the counter and hugged Lily.

"Wow, you look so much older, I heard you were in town. Has it been three years?"

"Yeah, it has, everything looks the same here except the pot section. It's good to see you."

"Are you buying flowers today?"

"Yeah, me and my friend Janet, the girl with the dark hair over by the geraniums. We're picking out flowers for Officer Cannon."

"Yeah, I heard what happened, word gets around quickly in this town. Is she ok?"

"She's doing well. She woke up this morning and the doctor said to take it easy and rest for a while."

"Well, that's good, are you guys ok? I heard about those psycho men trying to kill you both. That's pretty serious?"

"Jessie, how did you know about that?"

"Sergeant Jackson is my younger cousin. I saw him this morning and he was getting some flowers for her, too. He told me he thought you were very attractive."

Lily's face turned as pink as the tulips next to her, and excitement flew through her.

"Well, he's sweet. I think he is such a nice man."

"Maybe he'll ask you to go on a date sometime."

"Yeah, maybe. I like him, he's the nicest man I've met in a long time. Hey a gentleman. But, I should go help pick out some flowers. We still have to visit her then head over to the station later to talk to your cousin."

"Ok, by the way, the roses and petunias are fifty percent off today."

"Thank you, they do look beautiful."

"No problem."

Lily went over to Janet who had already picked out a handful of flowers. She had white and yellow lilies, pink geraniums, and a variety of different colored roses. Lily picked up some pink peonies and handed them to Janet to see what the bouquet looked like.

"I think that is good, unless you see another pretty flower," Lily told Janet.

"No, I think it looks beautiful and it's a really big bouquet. I don't think we can fit anymore in my hand if we wanted to."

Lily laughed and went over to pick out a vase from the shelves in the back of the shop. There were many vases, but the one that caught Lily's eye was a clear cube one. It was the perfect length and it was one of the more unique vases on the shelf. Janet was already at the check out paying for the flowers and chatting away with Jessie. Lily went to the front counter and placed the vase down for Jessie to ring it up.

"You guys did well making this bouquet. I love this flower combo!"

"Janet gets credit for that, she picked them out while we were talking."

"I did see her skimming through every row, picking up my favorites."

"Yeah, I couldn't make up my mind."

When Janet was finished paying, they thanked Jessie and Lily hugged her before walking out the door. Lily drove downtown to the hospital and pulled into the thirty-minute visitor parking. Janet opened her door and slid out of the car holding the vase in her hand. They walked up to the main entrance and then went to the front desk.

The woman sitting at the front counter was loud, calling people up to sign their medical forms. Lily asked the woman where Officer Cannon's room was, and the woman rolled her chair to the other side to open a big filing cabinet drawer with all the hospital patient records. She opened the first drawer labeled A-E and searched for Officer Cannon's file, scrolling through the tan folders with her fingers. She pulled out a folder and checked a paper that had all her information.

"She's in room 92."

"Thank you," Lily said as she left the front desk.

Lily pushed the second-floor button on the elevator and up they went.

"Elevators make me dizzy," Lily announced.

"I know my head feels weird, it always feels like the elevator isn't going anywhere. I especially don't like this one. When you were in the hospital the light kept flickering off and on, it freaked me out."

Lily closed her eyes and tried thinking of something to distract her mind. The elevator made a beep sound and opened up a second later. Janet and Lily stepped out looking at a room right across from them, room 81. Lily looked over to the right side to see what the next number was.

"That one is eighty, so let's go left."

Janet followed Lily, still carrying the vase of flowers in her hand. They turned down another hall to their right and room 92 was a few doors away. Lily opened the door and held it open for Janet. Officer Cannon was awake in her bed reading a book. There were flowers all around her room and some get-well balloons hanging from the end of the bed. She was wearing a buttoned-down white gown, and on the right side of her forehead was a large band-aid covering a large cut. Officer Cannon looked up and was surprised to see Lily and Janet standing in the doorway.

"Well, hello girls," she said, surprised.

   Janet walked over to the side of the bed and handed her the flowers for her to smell. She reached to grab the vase and buried her nose in the flowers smelling the sweet scent.

"Thank you, these smell so good and I love the flowers you picked out. Lilies are one of my favorites."

"Janet picked those out. Actually, she picked out most of them," Lily laughed.

   Janet grabbed the flowers and placed them down on the stand next to the bed.

"How are you feeling today?"

"I'm feeling sore. I can't move much yet, the doctor told me to stay in bed for a little while."

"Well, it's good to see you awake and ok. You were so brave to go into my father's house with those men in there."

"That's our job, to protect the community, and I'm glad you girls called us. You both could've been seriously hurt or killed."

Lily looked at Janet and pressed her lips together. She knew Officer Cannon was right, they needed to go home soon to avoid any more danger.

"We will be more careful, they still haven't found them. There are cops out today looking for them."

"That's good, I wish I could be out there. It's so boring sitting in this room for most of the day. But the Sergeant told me this morning he has an idea what they look like from the description you told him. They will be found."

"Well, we still have to visit the sergeant. He wanted to talk to us about something. We'll probably take off and let you rest," said Lily.

"Ok, thank you girls for coming to see me and bringing me these beautiful flowers. Stay safe and I hope I see you both before you leave back to California!"

"You're welcome! Feel better and we'll make sure to stop by before we leave," Janet said.

Lily and Janet opened the door and walked down the halls to the elevator. "I hope she feels better. I feel guilty since those men want us and we're getting other people in danger, as well."

"Well, Lily, like Officer Cannon said it's her job to protect and her job can be dangerous sometimes. Also, if you're also referring to the bomb at the restaurant, we had no idea that it would be in your dessert."

"Yeah, that was the last thing I expected to be in that cake. I was imagining some fudge or berries," Lily chuckled.

When they made it downstairs and got into the parking lot, Lily started the car and drove down the road to the station.

"I wonder what the Sergeant wants to give us?" Janet wondered.

"I don't know, but we're about to find out."

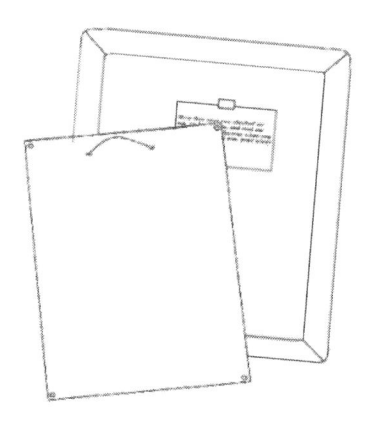

Chapter XIII
For Your Protection

Lily pulled into the police station and locked the car after getting out. They walked up to the front doors passing a few officers that just came out of the station.

"Thank you," Lily said to an officer holding the door open for them. Inside the station, there was a circular front desk and hallways leading to who knows where. You could see the black railing bordering the upstairs, and three big flags hanging down from the far wall behind the front desk.

Lily asked the man at the front desk if they could see Sergeant Jackson. The man asked for her name and called the sergeant from the front desk phone. He then stood up from his seat and told Janet and Lily to follow him up to Sergeant Jackson's office. They went down the hall and up the stairs, and when they were upstairs Lily and Janet looked over the railing. The whole first floor looked huge. People were walking all over the station, Lily could see an officer cuffing a prisoner before walking out of the doors. Owens' office was in the front of the building. The door had the words Sergeant O. Jackson at eye level in shining gold letters. The officer told them to go in and he walked back to the front desk. Lily opened the door and Sergeant Jackson was sitting at his desk looking at a paper in his hand.

"Oh, come on in."

Lily shut the door and they sat in the comfy black office chairs in front of his desk. The sergeant leaned back in his chair, "So, how was your shopping day? Find anything cool?"

"Yes, we found a few things, and Janet was amazed by the cylinder fish tank in my favorite shop."

"Oh yeah, that's the best souvenir shop to go to. They have all kinds of trinkets and gifts in there. That was the first shop I checked out when I moved here. So, you said you had a paper with one of their handwriting on it."

"Yes I have it in my purse," Lily said, pulling the paper out from a tiny pocket inside. She handed the paper to the Sergeant and he looked at the paper reading the message that was written in blue ink.

"We can check if it has fingerprints, the fastest results would be in an hour, so I'll call you or Janet to tell you if anything comes up."

"Thank you so much for your help! You've done so much for us."

"You're welcome, and I should give you the thing I mentioned before I forget."

He opened his desk drawer and pulled out two bracelets. They both looked the same: thick black thread and in the middle was a gray flat circle charm. He handed them to Lily and Janet for them to put around their small dainty wrists. Lily looked at the bracelet that was on her wrist and wondered why it was so important.

"These bracelets have trackers inside the charm. If one of you or both of you are in trouble, push the little button under the charm and we can find out where you are. You must wear these until we can locate these men."

"This is a smart idea and I already feel safer with this on," replied Janet. " I won't be as worried from now on if you know where we're at. He called for someone on his desk phone to come to get the note and told them to test it for any fingerprints. They told the sergeant they would need to get going before the library closed because it would take them a minute to find the next clue. Lily and Janet stood up, thanked Sergeant Jackson for everything, and said they would probably see him soon.

They were almost out of his office when he said, "Hey, Lily."

She turned around and told Janet to head down the stairs. Janet whispers in Lily's ear, "Tell me later!"

"Ok, go, " Lily told Janet as she pushed her out of the doorway.

Lily turned a shade pinker and her head was blowing up with too many thoughts. She didn't know what was going to happen. He slowly walked closer to her and reached over her to shut the door. He took her hand and led her over to his desk, then looked deeply into her eyes. With a gentle touch, he says "I can't hold it back any longer. I'm falling for you."

Lily's face turned an even brighter shade of pink. He took a deep breath and continued, "Every time we get together my heart races, and I think you are the most beautiful woman I've ever laid eyes on. I would love to get to know you better, and wanted to ask if you would like to go see a movie tonight?"

His words were like a warm embrace, wrapping around her heart and filling her with a sense of love and happiness. They were like a gentle breeze, carrying whispers of affection that danced through the air. Every word he said left her longing for more. Lily smiled and was thrilled to be asked.

"Yes, I would love that! I've only been to the movies like four times and only with friends!"

"Well, I can be your fifth time. I mean this will be your fifth time going," he corrects himself. "Sorry, that came out weird, I haven't really flirted with anyone since high school, really," he laughed.

"You're fine," Lily laughed back. "What time do you want to pick me up?"

"Let's say around six-thirty."

"That's perfect, I'll be ready. Do you think Janet should be at the house by herself?"

"I think she'll be fine, we'll be gone for just over two hours. But, if she feels safer staying with someone, I can call my older cousin and see if they can hang out."

"Jessie?"

"Yes, she said she knew you well and you said you were getting flowers today. I assume she met Janet."

"Yeah, they were talking away this morning and she would probably like that. I'll tell her and call you back to see what she says."

"Sounds good. I'll see you tonight, then."

"See you tonight."

Lily walked out of his office with a Cheshire cat smile, she was so excited to be going out with Owen. She looked down and could see Janet waiting by the front doors sitting in a chair similar to the one in Owen's office. Janet stood up and noticed Lily's pinkish face and a big smile.

"You won't believe what just happened."

"Ooh, you better give me every juicy detail! What did he say?"

"He asked me to go to the movies tonight at 6:30."

"That's so cute! Was he flirting with you?"

"Yeah, you could tell he hadn't done it in a while, but he was so funny and super sweet. He pulled me close to him, grabbed my hand, and his words just melted my heart."

"I feel like we're in high school," remarked Janet.

"I know and, by the way, he said if you don't feel comfortable staying at the house alone you can go over to Jessie's to hang out."

"Oh, that sounds fun. She doesn't mind?"

"No, he said to tell him and we'll let her know if you're coming over."

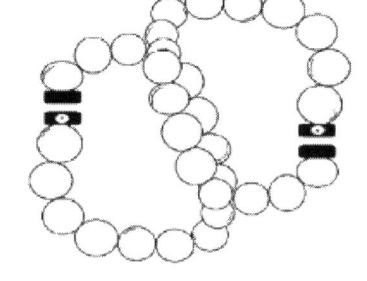

"Well, yeah, that would be fun."

"Ok, I'll call him in an hour because those results should be done and we'll both have some fun tonight."

They walked out of the station and Lily started the car.

Chapter XIV
Flying Books and Hide N' Seek

Lily and Janet walked into the library and it was just as Lily remembered. The floors were a light brown stained concrete, carpet in some reading corners with bean bags and comfy chairs. The movie and music section looked a little bigger than before, and she noticed more shelves of magazines. The walls had beautiful murals painted in the kid's section, which made the kid's area look enjoyable and exciting. There were different colored bean bags around every bookshelf corner and a huge globe in the middle of the room. There were different colors of origami cranes, hearts, fish, dogs, and butterflies hanging from the ceiling throughout the kid's section, lighting up the room with bright colors.

Lily's favorite part of the library was the extensive fireplace upstairs, with dark bricks and a shelf in the middle with small decorations placed on top. There were two bigger couches facing each other in front of the fireplace and a snug little chair in the middle. Janet looked at a paper on the wall that had the library hours.

"Lily, it's almost closing time."

"Oh, that's probably why there isn't anyone here. We better find it fast."

Lily and Janet split up to look for the book 'Julie Of The Wolves', Janet went to look in the children's section downstairs and Lily went upstairs.

"The children's section is smaller, so if it's not down here I'll come up to look upstairs with you," Janet said as she walked away from Lily.

"Ok, I'll be in one of the aisles upstairs."

Lily took the stairs and once she was upstairs she saw the aesthetic fireplace that she used to read by when she was younger. She looked around seeing no one in sight, there were only two people in a study room by the stairs about to walk out.

She started to look up at the labels on top of the bookshelves. Passing: food and cooking, art and design, mystery, romance, science fiction, fantasy, historical fiction, biography, and sports. Lily walked down the novel aisle hoping it would be there and it would be an easy find. She ran her finger along the book spines searching for the author's last name in bold print. She looked through the C's and didn't see the book anywhere.

Lily went towards the back looking for the fiction section, thinking it would be there. She looked up and down the fiction aisle and finally found the book after twenty minutes. Lily pulled the book out from the shelf and checked inside, flipping through the pages to see if anything was shoved in or written. She didn't see anything, no note and no writing on any of the pages. Excitement turned into confusion. Why was nothing inside the book? She was positive this was the next clue.

She had an idea, Lily bent down and reached her hand back behind the books where the 'Julie Of The Wolves' was. She felt something squared, Lily pulled it out from behind the books and looked at the object she just pulled out, it was an envelope. The envelope felt heavier and bumpy at the bottom.

"This has to be it," Lily said out loud.

A woman smiled as she walked by and went to the back of the library. Lily puts the book back where she found it and shoves the envelope into her purse. As she was putting the envelope in her purse she felt a nervous cold shiver in her body. She looked over to the left, a man was leaning up against the bookshelf staring at Lily with his arms crossed.

"Need help finding anything?" asked the man.

Lily stared at the man for a second before answering.

"No, thank you, I was just leaving," Lily said in a slow tone.

"Are you sure, Miss Davis?"

Lily's eyes got bigger, she knew it was one of them, one of the younger accomplices of the man with different colored eyes. How did they know we were here? She thought to herself. He started to walk slowly towards Lily, but Lily didn't move. She was scared. Her mind told her to run, but her body wouldn't move. She looked over and in a space in the bookshelf next to her she saw another man, but this man made her body shake in fear. He had dark brown hair, one eye was misty gray and the other a green-yellow. It was the man with different colored eyes.

"Nice to see you again," the man said in his deep voice, peeking through the empty shelf space.

"What do you want from me? Just leave us alone," Lily cried in fear. She started to back up. There were now two of them and only one of her.

"Our boss would love to have a little talk with you and if you come with us now we won't hurt your friend," the man in front of her said as he got closer.

Oh my god, Janet is downstairs, she thought. She needed to get away. She looked at the men one last time and started to run as fast as she could.

She had a head start, but Lily could hear their footsteps from afar getting louder as they came closer. Lily knew they were right behind her. Her chest was pounding, scared for her life, and took long strides running towards the stairs that led down to the first floor. She stopped and hid behind a bookshelf for just a second, almost breathless from running. Lily perked her head up and listened, it was so dead silent that you could hear a pin drop. She looked over to the right side, then to the left. Where are they? She thought nervously. Lily could see the stairs from where she stood and wanted to make a run for it. She looked behind her and the men were running towards her.

She ran down an aisle with the men right behind her. She grabbed two random thick books quickly off the shelf and threw them at the men, hitting one square in the face and one hit the other man's leg. The man fell back from getting hit in the face and the other man tripped over him. Lily ran out of the aisle hearing one of them yell at the other.

"Get off me and get that twit, you idiot!"

She ran over to a corner with a big rocking chair and hid behind it. She was terrified and didn't know how to get downstairs without being seen. Lily stayed crouched down behind the chair for a few minutes trying to come up with a working plan, a plan that would get her out of this.

Lily peaked over the chair and she could see the men lurking around the library. She ducked down and thought of a plan that might work.

She murmured to herself, "Please work, please work, please work."

She quietly grabbed a book that was sitting on a shelf next to the chair and threw it in the air. The book made a loud clunk, the men turned around and jogged toward the sound. Lily saw her chance to run to the elevator which was closer than the stairs. Lily ran over to the elevator and pressed the button to open the elevator. The elevator opens slowly and Lily goes in and hits the first floor button a few times before it starts to close. The two men came around the corner and saw Lily in the elevator. They both run to the closing elevator, but before they could reach Lily the elevator closes shut.

Lily has a sigh of relief and waits anxiously for the door to open. All Lily could think about was finding Janet and getting out of the library. When the door opens Lily could see a few strangers picking out movies and a couple of people in some aisles. Lily casually jogged to a far corner across from the kid's section looking to see if Janet was still in there. She saw something in the corner of her eye, it was the men coming down the stairs.

Lily crouched down and kept looking for any sign of Janet. Lily became worried and was thinking the worst in her head, like if they kidnapped Janet or had already hurt her and Lily didn't know. Lily was watching for the men, making sure they didn't find her and at the same time she was looking for Janet.

"It has been ten minutes, where is she?" Lily whispered to herself.

She was so focused on looking at the kid's section that she didn't realize someone was standing behind her. Lily felt a hand on her shoulder and freaked out. She was about to scream but the person put her hand over Lily's mouth and crouched down to Lily's level.

"Oh my god, Janet you scared me to death!"

"What are you doing?" Janet asked, confused. "Are you playing hide n' seek, because I've been looking for you?"

"Looking for me? I've been looking for you for like ten minutes," Lily whispered back. "Ok, follow me and don't stand completely up," Lily told Janet.

Lily led Janet to the back of the library where no one was at.

"Ok, you want to tell me what's going on?" asked Janet.

"Ok, the men are here."

"Oh my god, how did they know we were here?"

"I don't know, but I got a good look at them and they talked to me upstairs. They both wanted me to come with them to talk with their boss. I told them something, then ran as fast as I could downstairs."

"I should've been with you! I'm glad you're alright. Did you get the clue?"

"Yes, I haven't looked at it yet. I wanted to wait for you."

"So, how do we get out of here without being seen and followed?"

"I had an idea when I was upstairs hiding. Let's sneak by the front doors and see if it's clear first."

Janet and Lily peeked up from the bookshelf, looking to see if any of the men were in sight. They moved quietly and cautiously with every step, making their way to the front doors. Lily notices the two men sitting on a bench by the doors, pretending to read magazines.

"Oh crap, how are we going to get out?" asked Janet.

" I saw an exit door beside the bathrooms, but we could possibly be seen."

"Well, we don't have a choice."

Janet and Lily went back a few aisles across the bathrooms and waited for the right moment.

"You ready? Just don't make a big scene and if we see them get up, we make a run for it," Lily told Janet.

"Yes, I'm ready, I've got the keys already in my hand."

Lily casually walked out from the aisle going to the exit door then Janet followed. They were only a couple seconds from the aisle and one man had seen them. The two men stood up and Lily's eyes met one of theirs. Lily kept moving, staring at the man's face and whispering to Janet one word, run. Janet sprinted to the exit doors and they could hear the men's heavy footsteps coming at them, but Lily and Janet were already out the emergency door.

Janet started the car and Lily jumped in the passenger seat. Janet drove off and out of the parking lot, and Lily turned around looking for any cars following them.

"That was just too close," Janet said breathlessly.

"When are they going to give up?"

"I don't know, but I do feel safer with these bracelets on," Lily replied.

"That was seriously one of the scariest times of my life, getting chased upstairs. I mean the bomb was terrifying at the restaurant, but I was alone and scared standing right next to them. I still remember those horrifying eyes staring into me reading me, like a book, trying to figure out what I'll say or do next."

"I should've stayed with you. You need to be with someone at all times when we're out. Who knows what will happen next, they seem to pop out of nowhere."

"Well, it's over now. Pull over somewhere, I'm really curious about what's inside that envelope," said Lily.

Janet pulled into Jack's Pizza restaurant and parked the car under a nice healthy thick-leaved tree. Lily checked if the coast was clear and then pulled the weighted envelope out of her purse. She ripped the top of the envelope and looked inside.

"What's inside, Lily? Another note?"

"Yes, there's a note and another key. I thought it seemed a little heavy."

Janet grabbed the key from Lily and looked at the engraved details. A long dock leads to ocean waters and a sun shines in the background.

"This is really beautiful. Your father must've gotten it specially made."

"Yeah, it is gorgeous."

She opened the note and read the few words on the paper.

"The key is the clue," Lily said puzzled.

She grabbed the key out of Janet's hand and looked at it closely.

"I think he's telling us to go to one of the docks."

"Well, how many are there?" asked Janet.

"Three that I know of. Two by the lighthouse, and one a couple of miles near my father's house."

"What are we waiting for? Let's go to the lighthouse first. We have a couple hours of daylight left."

"Yeah, might as well. I'll drive since I know where it is. I have a feeling we're getting closer."

   Lily and Janet got out of the car and swapped seats, so Lily could drive to the lighthouse and find the next clue before the day runs out. She drove out of the parking lot and looked both ways and behind her.

"You don't see the BMW or the Mercedes anywhere, do you?" Asked Lily.

Janet checked her mirror, "No, I don't see anyone. But how excited are you to go on your date?"

"I'm really excited and also nervous. He's a wonderful guy, I just don't want to say anything stupid, you know what I mean?"

"Yeah, when I was a freshman in college I went out with this one dude. He had blonde hair and blue eyes. It went great at first. We went bowling and laughed the whole time at dinner. Then I had to go to the bathroom and I also wanted to reapply my lipstick.

"Oh my god, Janet," Lily laughed. "Did you have lipstick on your face?"

"No, close, I walked out and started talking for twenty minutes and he never told me I had lipstick on my teeth!"

"Wow, some date."

"Well, the thing is, he saw it and didn't tell me for the whole dinner. It was so embarrassing for the waiter to tell me I had red lipstick on my teeth."

Lily was laughing at Janet so hard that she missed the next turn to the lighthouse.

"Crap! You distracted me. Is anyone behind us?"

Janet turned around to double-check after looking in her mirror, "Nope."

"Perfect, I'm just going to back up, and go down the right road."

A few minutes later, Lily pulled into a long dirt road that led to the lighthouse. Janet rolled down her window and could hear the cool waves rush up into the gritty hot sand. They finally arrived and could see the tall lighthouse standing strong up on the small hill. The lighthouse was still charming, white with a few red and blue horizontal stripes wrapping around it. The only thing that has changed was the light on top. The lighthouse was still in fine shape for it being around ninety-five years old.

"It looks so quiet and peaceful out here," Janet said to Lily.

"I know. I forgot how pretty it is. I love listening to the ocean waters splashing on rocks."

They hopped out of the car and started walking down the trail to the lighthouse. When they got there, Janet read an engraved message on the lighthouse wall.

"Brewer Lighthouse Built by Mike Brewer and his wife Le Etta Brewer In 1896."

"So, where do you want to start?" Asked Janet.

"There's two docks. Let's check the furthest one first and make our way to the dock by the lighthouse."

"Sounds good to me. What exactly are we looking for again?"

"I'm not sure. The key just shows a dock, so we'll just look near it or maybe in the water."

Janet and Lily walked a few minutes to the furthest dock and started looking around. Lily went to the end of the dock and stared at the ocean. She looked down, hoping there was some carved writing on the peer, but there wasn't. Nowhere in sight did she see what looked like a clue. It had to be somewhere else.

Lily turned around, "Janet did you find anything yet ?"

"No, I didn't find anything that didn't look out of place or wasn't supposed to be there. I looked at that massive tree over there with carvings all over it. I didn't see anything but names, phone numbers, and dates."

"I didn't find anything either. I think we should check the other dock, I have a feeling there's one there."

The girls walked to the furthest dock first and tried searching the area. Janet checked the rocks, making sure nothing was tucked or underneath something. She checked in the sand for any possible boxes or notes. Lily went to the end of the dock and once again checked for any writings, or carvings on the wood, and then checked in the water. The water was clean and the ocean ground was visible. The water was so clear Lily could see sea shells in the sand and some white coral a little bit passed the dock. She then walked back to the dock by the Brewer Lighthouse. She sat down, took off her shoes, and dipped her feet in the ocean waving them around in the warm water. Janet came up beside Lily and sat next to her, doing the same thing Lily was doing.

"Aah, this is relaxing. I wish it was like this every day, this view is gorgeous."

"I know, I would love to move back here someday, if no one kills me before we leave."

Janet laughed, "Don't worry about it, we're in safe hands. They still have cops out searching and we have these bracelets on now. If anything happens, the cops will know, and they'll know where to find us."

"You know, I used to come here sometimes and think about things. Last time I was here was when my mom died."

Janet wrapped her arm around Lily and hugged her tight. Lily closed her eyes and listened to the sound of the waves applauding and hugging the shore. Janet grabbed a pebble that was left on the dock behind her and threw it into the deep blue sea.

"We can sit here a few minutes and then drive to the third dock," Lily suggested.

"Yeah, we want to make it back in time for your date tonight," Janet laughed.

"I'm just going to see a movie."

Janet giggled and threw a smaller pebble than before into the sea before walking back to the lighthouse. Lily was mesmerized by the ripples from her foot in the water. She stared at them for a minute and something caught her eye. A thin rope was tied to a post underneath the deck.

"Hey, Janet!"

"Yeah?"

"There's this rope tied to this post. I'm going to pull it up and see what is at the other end!"

"Yeah, let's see what's tied to it," Janet said as she jogged back.

Lily got on her knees and reached into the water and started pulling the rope up.

"It's nothing that heavy," said Lily.

Lily could see a blurry object coming up and getting clearer. It was a bottle with a rock tied to it for weight. She lifted the bottle and set it on the dock.

"It's a bottle."

"I thought it would be something else like a fish cage," said Janet.

"This is it, this is the clue we were supposed to find1 I see a small piece of paper inside the bottle," Lily said excitedly.

"It looks well sealed. I'm going to throw it on the dock and shatter it. Better watch out," Lily warned Janet.

Janet stood up and watched Lily throw the bottle. The bottle shattered everywhere into tiny pieces, and the white paper was lying on the dock waiting for Lily to pick it up.

"Don't cut yourself," said Janet.

"I won't. Come over here and I'll read it."

Janet walked over carefully, trying not to step on any glass. Lily unfolded the paper and read the words her father wrote for her.

"At night I shine my bright light on the earth's deep waters, signaling sailors so they can return home safely." *

"Well, we don't have to go very far for the next clue. It's the lighthouse," said Lily.

Janet looked at the old rustic lighthouse and pointed to the top. "Let's go up there and find it then."

Janet started running to the lighthouse and waved at Lily telling her to hurry up. When they both reached the lighthouse, Lily opened the white creaking door.

"Looks like no one's home, let's head up those stairs," Lily said.

"Good."

Janet and Lily made their way up the metal stairs, making loud noises on each step. Lily opened a hatch door and the first thing she saw was the rail at the top, going around the lighthouse, and the light in the center.

The light was big, bulky, and was protected by a glass box, keeping it safe from weather. The glass box had a lock on the door, making it difficult to get inside without a key.

"How are we going to open this Janet?"

"Do you have your knife?"

"No."

She opened her purse and grabbed the key with the dock engraved on top. "I bet it's this key."

"Oh yeah, I kinda forgot about that key."

Lily grabbed the lock, put the key in the hole, and turned the key. It clicked and Lily took the key out of the hole.

"Yes! Good job, Lily," said Janet.

"Thanks, now where is the clue?"

Lily looked at the light and didn't see much. She saw a warning note on the inside of the door, then looked down and saw something. There was a note lying at the bottom of the light box.

"I found it, but it's kinda far down," said Lily as she tried to reach for it.

"Ok, I can get it. I just have to reach a little further."

Lily reached her arm down the tight slot. She could feel the note touching her fingertips, but couldn't get it. Her armpit was starting to feel numb from reaching down so long. She couldn't reach any further, but felt the edge of the note with her middle finger. Lily was finally able to reach the note and pulled her arm out.

"That feels better. You want to read it, Janet?"

Janet laughed, "Yeah, I'll let you shake the blood back in your arm."

She gave the note to Janet to read and Lily rubbed her arm to stop the numbness. Janet opened the note and read out loud.

"Dear Lily,

You've done an amazing job, now go to the old mine in the woods. When you're inside, follow these directions: left, right, right. Be careful, these mines are old and abandoned. Anything could happen. And just remember what I said, don't trust anyone and keep the knife with you at all times and never know when you'll need it. *

Be safe, love, father"

"So, the next clue is in the mines," said Lily.

"I haven't been there since I was a kid. They shut it down from a tunnel collapse that killed two men a couple of years back. What was in his mind telling him to put the clue in there?"

"Well, that's just nice of your father for sending us in there," Janet said dramatically.

"If he put the next clue in there, he probably made sure the tunnels were safe enough to be in," said Lily.

"Yeah, you're probably right. Let's go tomorrow, the sun is going to set soon. What time is it?"

Lily looked down at her watch and read the time.

"It's 5:30, you want me to drive home?"

"Yeah, if you want to."

Lily and Janet walked back down the stairs and shut the door to the lighthouse. The drive back didn't take long, only a couple minutes from the lighthouse to Lily's father's house.

"I think you should wear your yellow dress tonight. I think he'll like it," Janet suggested.

"I'll try it on, but I'm not sure what I want to wear."

Lily pulled into the driveway just before the sun started to set. They unlocked the door and went inside the house to get ready for the night.

"I'm going upstairs to change into something more comfortable. Are you coming up too?" Janet asked.

"I'll be going up in a moment."

Lily sat down at the kitchen table and read the note in her hand again. She placed it on the table and took off her bracelet Owen gave to her. She rubbed her wrist and rushed upstairs to get ready for her date.

Lily took a quick shower and, afterwards, opened her closet door and looked at the clothes she packed. It was a choice between the yellow dress Janet suggested or a longer flirty green dress that had a ruffled top. She held them both up to her body and picked the green dress. Lily brushed her long hair and curled the ends. Janet walked in with leggings and a t-shirt ready for a night of fun with Jessie.

"You look so pretty, Lily! Now if that man doesn't fall in love with you tonight, then I will give him a piece of my mind."

"Well, you'll find out when I get back. He should be here soon, we decided 6:30 and it's 6:10 right now. You can go to Jessie's house if you want. Her house is the greenhouse behind the bank."

"Are you sure? I don't want to leave you here alone, Lily."

"It's ok. He'll be picking me up in like twenty minutes."

Janet cocked her head and raised her eyebrows, giving Lily that 'mom look'.

"I promise I'll be careful and I'll give him a call in a few minutes."

"Ok, I'll leave. Just call me when you're coming home and I'll leave her house."

"You got it, have fun," said Lily.

"I will, you go kill it. I want all the juicy details when I get home."

Janet laughed and walked out of Lily's bedroom, and out the door. Lily could hear the car leave the driveway as she was finishing her hair. She was now all alone in the house. As she was putting her earrings in, she heard the phone ring downstairs. Lily jogged down the stairs while trying to put her second earring in. She picked up the phone and answered.

"Hello?"

"Hey Lily, it's Owen. Are you at the house?"

He sounded different over the phone. His voice was a bit deeper, but still made Lily blush.

"Yes, I'm getting ready. Are you on your way?"

"Oh, yes, and I have something to tell you when I get there."

"Ok I'll be done getting ready by the time you get here," said Lily as she walked back up the stairs to finish getting ready.

"I'll be there in a few minutes."

   He hung up and Lily put some mascara on and put the phone on the bed. A few minutes later she heard a car pull into the driveway. Excitement ran through Lily as she put on some light lipstick. She made sure it couldn't get on her teeth and went to the closet to get her purse. Lily heard a car door shut lightly and then she heard another. That confused her. She took slow steps over to the window and saw something she wished she hadn't seen. There was a black BMW parked in the driveway, and men trying to enter the house. Lily couldn't believe what she was seeing. What was she going to do?

Chapter XV

Taken

   Lily's heart thundered in her chest. She saw the phone on the bed and called Owen's number.

"Come on pick up! Pick up."

"Hey, I'm almost on my way."

   Lily cut him off before he could finish.

"Owen, they're her! They're coming for me, don't let them take me!"

   Lily was sobbing as she told Jackson. She was scared for her life and realized she left her bracelet downstairs on the kitchen table, but it was too late to grab it.

"Ok, Lily I'm coming but you're going to have to hide. Where are you?"

"I'm in my room upstairs."

"Is Janet there with you?"

"No, she left ten minutes ago to go to Jessie's house. Owen, I'm scared."

She heard a window shatter downstairs and started to freak out even more.

"I heard a window shatter. They are breaking in."

"Ok, listen to everything I say, Lily. You need to get under the bed and stay as quiet as you can."

Lily quickly went into her purse to grab the pocket knife that her father left for her and placed it inside her bra. She dropped down on her stomach and slid under the bed breathing quieter.

"Ok, I'm under the bed."

"Good, now listen, they're probably going to take you. I need you to keep as quiet as possible so I can listen."

Lily knew he was right. They were going to take her and it could be the last time she talked to Owen. She could hear the door open and heavy footsteps were going around the house.

"Owen, they're in here. They're coming," Lily whispered.

"I am recording everything and I am almost four minutes away. Everything will be ok and I promise I will find you. I won't stop until I find you, understand me?"

"Yes, just stay with me ok."

Lily could hear footsteps quickly coming up the stairs. She shed a tear and could hear them talking. She was frightened for her life and heard them walk into Janet's room. Then she could see two pairs of boots walking right up to her bed. Lily closed her eyes and prayed. She opened them and saw the pair of boots walk out of the room. The room was silent. Lily wasn't sure if both men had left the room or just one. She had only seen one man walk out of her bedroom, but she didn't see nor hear anyone. Lily gently put the phone on the floor and turned her head to look again one more time.

She whispered into the phone, "Owen, I think they're downstairs."

"Ok, don't move I'm almost," Sargent Jackson was interrupted by Lily screaming over the phone.

"Aaaaaaaaaaaaah!"

A man was standing behind her and pulled her out from under the bed by grabbing her feet. Her piercing cry broke Owen's heart, why is this happening? Her cry forced him to go at least seventy miles an hour down the road to get to Lily. The man grabbed Lily and forced her upwards. He called downstairs for his partner, who was searching in the kitchen.

Lily struggled to get out of his grip, it was too late to get away now. The younger man pushed Lily face down on the bed and tied her hands together.

"Stay still!"

The man shouted at Lily, who was sobbing on the bed crying for help. She heard the other man coming up the stairs. Lily looked to her left and standing in the doorway was the man with different colored eyes.

"Well, hello hot stuff. Hiding from us? Where's your friend, Janet, hiding?"

"She's gone, you just missed her," Lily snapped back.

"Well then, we can leave now. Put her in the car," he ordered.

The younger man yanked Lily up onto her feet and forced her out of the house. Lily had to get away. Who knows what would happen to her.

Right when Lily stepped out of the front door with a gun held to her head, she stomped on the man's foot as hard as she could, turned around, and kicked him in the stomach. The man fell back onto the ground. Lily started to make a run for it, but another man came out from the back of the BMW and grabbed Lily.

She screamed, but it was no use. The man slapped his hand over her mouth and pulled her into the BMW with some help from the man she just kicked.

Lily was so close. So close to getting away, but there were too many of them to take on her own.

The man with the different colored eyes jumped into the BMW and the driver drove off fast, passing the speed limit to a number Lily didn't want to see. Lily sat in the middle of two men in the back seat. Her heart was still racing to the point where it was hard to breathe. The younger man gave the other a torn rag and he tied it tight over Lily's mouth. Lily didn't struggle, she was scared but couldn't let that show. The younger man knelt and tied Lily's ankles together. Lily tried to kick him again, but he had a tight grip on both ankles.

"Ain't getting away now, girly. You aren't going anywhere!"

Lily didn't like the way he said that last part. In her mind she had a few ideas of what that part would lead to later on. She saw the man up front dial a number on the phone and put it up to his ear.

"Yeah, boss, we have her. We'll be there in twenty minutes. We're taking the back roads, I'm expecting cops to be everywhere. Ok, boss."

He hung up and told the man to slow down so they didn't look suspicious. In Lily's mind, she wanted to know who their boss was and why he wanted her dead so badly. Lily was uncomfortable and frightened, and being in her worst nightmare tied up next to the men who had tried to kill her multiple times in the last few days, made her stomach ache. All these thoughts went into her head: 'how can I get out of this car?' 'What will happen to me?' 'What do these men want?' 'Will I ever see Janet again?' 'Why do they want me dead?' The thoughts never ended in Lily's head, she was almost going insane.

It's been about five minutes in this car Lily thought. Lily looked out the windows to see where they were going. It was dark, but Lily could tell she was going past the barber shop. The man with the different colored eyes, turned around to check on Lily. He realized she was looking out the window and told the man to knock her out with chloroform. She struggled and fought to stay awake, but it worked into her a minute or two later.

Back at the house, Janet pulled in to grab something she had forgotten. She saw the door wide open and a broken window shattered. Janet started to freak out and knew something was wrong. Carefully, she pushed the door open wider and peaked before going inside. Janet looked down and saw a large stick laying by the door. She picked it up, held it like a baseball bat, and walked through the front entrance. Janet looked around for any sign of Lily.

"LILY!" Janet shouted.

"LILY!" Janet shouted again.

Janet ran around the house looking for Lily, and upstairs, no Lily.

"Why did I leave her?"

Janet dropped the stick and started to break down. She fell back against the wall and slid down. Tears landed on her knees and slid down her leg. She lifted her head and saw the phone under Lily's bed. She quickly grabbed it and knew Lily was hiding under the bed when they found her. She then heard a car pulling into the driveway. Janet sat up, looked out Lily's window, and saw Owen. This was the second time the door was open when he pulled in. Owen grabbed his gun out of his glove department and ran up the driveway into the house without any hesitation.

"LILY! JANET!" Owen yelled.

He ran around downstairs checking every room.

"Up here, Owen," said Janet.

Owen ran upstairs and Janet met him at the top.

"Are you alright?" asked Sergeant Jackson.

"Yes, I just got here. They took Lily I'm guessing not long ago."

"I know she called me and I was driving as fast as I could to get here."

"Owen, what are we going to do?"

Owen grabbed the phone from Janet and dialed the Chief.

"I'm going to call my boss and get some men driving around town right now. I want you to stay with me. We're going to find her together."

"Yeah, that's a good idea. I don't want to be alone."

"Well, let's go. I can find Lily's location from the bracelets, but we have to do that in the car."

"We'll find her. I just hope she's not hurt."

Janet and Owen went quickly to his cop car and buckled in. He turned on his computer and searched to find Lily's location from her bracelet. Janet looked over at the computer and was fascinated by the technology. Owen pointed to the screen and looked at Janet.

"Ok, you see that blue dot right there?"

"Yes!"

"That's where you are and…" Owen paused, what he was seeing on the screen wasn't what he wanted to see. At that moment his stomach had felt like he swallowed a pit from an avocado.

"What? What's wrong?"

"Lily's dot is next to yours!"

Owen jumped out of the car and went back inside the house. Janet followed him to see what he was doing. Owen looked around the living room and then into the kitchen and saw it. Janet was out of breath from running after him.

"What are you looking for?" asked Janet.

   He grabbed the bracelet from off the table and turned around to show Janet.

"Lily doesn't have her bracelet on. We can not track her," Owen said in a slow and concerned tone.

"Oh my god, I heard her take a shower. She must've forgotten to put it back on. Owen, how are we going to find her?"

"We'll just have to search every part of this town."

   They went back to the car and Owen called the station as he drove out of the driveway.

"I think we should check the airport first to make sure they weren't planning on taking her somewhere else."

"That sounds like a good start. Owen, I couldn't live with myself if anything happened to her."

"We will find her. Every cop is out right now searching and I won't stop searching until she's found," said Owen.

   The chloroform wore off and Lily opened her eyes. She looked out the window and saw dark trees everywhere. She didn't know where she was. "Look who's awake, perfect timing," said the younger man.

Lily didn't know how long she was out, but was glad she was awake to see where she was at. The man stopped the car and opened his door. He went to the right side and moved what looked like some brush that covered a driveway. He jumped back in and drove the car into the drive then covered the entrance back up again. A secret driveway, now that's just great, Lily thought in her head.

He then drove down a driveway. It felt like it never ended, the woods were so dark and creepy. She then could see a few lights up ahead. It was a house at the end of the driveway, a beautiful house. She could see the details when they were closer. The house was all brick, had a second floor, and many windows. But it was far from the road and Lily didn't like that. Lily couldn't go inside that house, once she went in, she had a feeling that she wouldn't come out. Lily had to run for it when they took her out of the car, it was her only chance of escape.

She saw the Mercedes parked by the garage and then looked at the man sitting next to her. He gave her a crooked smile and nodded. Lily felt the car stop and was instantly shaken up. The man next to Lily took his knife out and cut her ankles free.

The same man grabbed Lily's chin, "Now, you are going give us no trouble going inside the house. No tricks and no screaming. No one is going to hear your screams this far into the woods."

The younger man grabbed Lily's arm and pulled her out of the car. Before the other man could come around the car, she stepped on the man's foot, punched him in the stomach with both tied hands, and ran. The man groaned on the ground and saw a cut on his arm. He cut himself with the knife when he fell to the ground. The man cursed at Lily and started cleaning his cut with his shirt.

"Get her, you half-wits," yelled the man with the different colored eyes.

Lily bought herself enough time to run into the woods and hope they didn't find her. Having dark woods to go into was a blessing. It was the perfect cover she needed. Lily didn't stop running, she knew they were right behind her. Lily rubbed the cloth off her mouth so it was easier to breathe while running. It was endless woods. Lily could run forever, but she had to hide them out and untie her hands. She grabbed a sharp stick and hid in some thick bushes hoping they were thick enough to keep her hidden. It took her a good minute to untie her hands, but she eventually broke free, thanks to the knife she had hid in her bra. Lily pulled the rope off her hands and suddenly heard talking near her. She saw two or three flashlights coming towards her. Lily stayed still and heard them talking, then they ran off in different directions.

Lily sat for a few minutes and then decided to get out of her hiding spot and make a run for it towards the road. That was the worst decision she had made. Lily crawled out of the bush and, before she was able to stand up, she was pushed to the ground. They found her, the man with different colored eyes had his foot on Lily and had a gun pointing down at her.

"She's over here, boys," yelled the man. "Now, you aren't going anywhere girl, make one more move and tonight won't be pleasant."

Three more men came and it was impossible to escape now. The younger man walked up with a wave of anger and kicked Lily's left side. The kick was hard and put a sharp pain instantly in her side. A man lifted her off the ground and held a rag over her mouth. Lily tried not to breathe in the chloroform on the rag, but it smelled stronger than last time.

Her vision started to fade and soon her eyes would close shut. Lily felt tired and woozy and didn't feel like fighting anymore, she had no more energy. A man picked Lily up and threw her over his shoulder and hiked back to the house. The last thing Lily saw that night was the back of the man's shoes and lights shining everywhere around her.

Chapter XVI
The Truth

   Lily started dreaming. It was the same dream she had a few days ago. The same dream that had haunted her since she was a little girl.

   She could see her father and mother out by the lake. They were laying down a picnic blanket to set up for lunch, while Lily played in the meadow-attempting to catch butterflies. They ate lunch and Lily's father took her to fish and talk by the lake. She remembered him telling her to never fully trust anybody because it might hurt you later on in life. He always said that to Lily and she could never figure out why until now. Lily was only a girl around the age of seven, the night she remembered screams coming from her parent's bedroom and fierce yelling. She pulled her yellow bunny close to her for protection and watched her bedroom door open closely. Lily saw a man come into her bedroom with a gun pointed down. It was dark and she couldn't see the details on his face, but could tell he had dark hair. The man wore a leather jacket and dark jeans.

He paused in the doorway and then walked towards Lily's bed. She pulled the covers tight to her and started to cry for her father. Lily remembered the man reaching for her about to take her out of her bed and then saw her father behind him. He hit the man on the head, the man dropped to the ground and Lily's father then took his gun from his hand. Her dream had gone farther than ever before. She remembered her father pointed the gun at the man and said "Deven, you've gone mad, I want you to get out and never come back to this house again. Leave my family alone. I'm not giving it to you and you'll never get it."

He gave me one last look and her father escorted him out of the house. He looked familiar, like Lily's seen him before multiple times. The dream ended with Lily's father holding her saying it was alright. It was a memory that wouldn't leave her mind, and why it came back to her now she didn't know. She did know that it was nice to see her parent's faces again, clear as crystal in her mind.

Her dream faded away and when Lily opened her eyes she was blinded by all the lights in the room. She felt like she had been sleeping for hours and could feel an ache in her side and her wrists. Lily looked around. She was in a big bedroom. The maroon drapes were closed, there was a small couch in front of the tv, a bathroom was connected to the room, and a corner fireplace was going. Lily tried to get up, but her wrists were tied to the bed and her ankles were zip-tied together. Lily tried to untie her right hand by bending her fingers, but it wouldn't work. Stuck on the bed, she listened to the crackle of the fire.

Lily just stared at the ceiling thinking how hopeless it was to get away. She made two attempts to escape and still ended up back where she started.

Lily looked around the room to find anything that would help her escape later on if she was still alive. There was a glass bowl with fruit on a round table she could shatter on someone's head. She could escape out the window if she wasn't tied up. The only sharp object was the fire poker beside the fireplace. Lily kept thinking of ideas on how to get out of the room, but her thoughts ended when the door opened. It was the man with different colored eyes. He shut the door and walked towards the bed with his hands in his pockets.

"Morning, hot stuff. I see you're finally awake," the man said as he made his way towards Lily.

"How long was I out?"

"A couple of hours, I had to knock you out so you wouldn't try anything funny again."

He sat on the bed beside Lily and put his hand on her thigh. He moved his hand up her thigh and started kissing her neck. Lily felt disgusted and tried to move her head to stop him from kissing her, but there wasn't much she could do. It only made him kiss her harder. His wet lips moved from her neck and up to her mouth. But he stopped when the door opened. Two men walked into the room and told the man on the bed that the boss wanted to see her.

"Alright, help me untie her, then."

The three men un-tied her wrists, cut the zip tie around her ankles, and pulled Lily off the bed. Two of the men took Lily by the arms and walked her out of the room at a quick pace. The men's grips were firm and their nails dug into the backs of Lily's arms, creating purple dents. Lily was examining the layout of the house so she could make an escape plan and hopefully use that plan later on. She walked through a long hallway and then down the stairs. She could then hear talking downstairs in a room that was lit up from the fireplace. She could see the shadows of her enemies on the ceiling and didn't want to go any further.

She looked at the windows and saw it was still dark out, but not as dark as before. The sun will be coming up soon. Lily pulled back and told the two men they were hurting her arms, but that just made them want to grip harder and when they entered the room they threw her down to the floor. Lily gasped and was slightly relieved because her arms were now free to breathe.

The man with different colored eyes took Lily by the hair and forced her head up. Lily tried to fight back but he grabbed the back of her neck to keep her from moving an inch. Lily was sitting on her legs and could already feel the blood being cut off. The man came closer to Lily and she could feel his body pressed up against her back. While a man tied Lily's wrists in front of her she looked around the room. A man stood watching by the window to her left, two men were standing in the archway of the room to her right, the man with different colored eyes was standing behind Lily and another man was tying her wrists together. In all, five men were watching Lily like a cougar watching its prey, ready to attack at any moment.

And another man stood in front of the fireplace watching the bright fire. He had dark hair and wore a black dress shirt with dark blue jeans. This must be him, Lily thought. She desperately wanted to know who he was. She wanted to see the face of the man that had been trying to destroy her life.

The moment of truth, the man turned around and when Lily saw him her heart dropped into her stomach. The last time she saw this man was in 1974. He was her father's best friend. It all came back to her when she saw his face again. Lily could remember some memories of him coming over every once in a while to have dinner or to hang out with her father. He was like an uncle to her.

"Hello, Lillian. Remember me?" The man said in a deep voice.

"Uncle Deven, you're the one who wants me dead?" Lily said in shock. "I always wondered what happened to you. You were so close with my father, and I remember you were always around when I was little. Why all this?"

"Yes, me and your father have known each other since we were kids. That night when you were seven is when everything changed. It was when your father betrayed me."

"You are the man in my dreams?" Lily was shocked, and that made her even more scared.

"He would never betray you, he loved you like his own brother!" Lily yelled.

"Yes, we were close. I grew up with your father and we both worked in the mines together for years. My parents both died when I was young and your grandparents took me in. When he married your gorgeous mother, you were born not long after. When we worked in the mines I got lucky in 74, and found a chunk of gold bigger than my hand. It was an unbelievable nugget. We were supposed to give anything we found to the company, but I wanted it for myself, I had to have it. I showed your father the nugget I discovered because he was the only one I trusted, but that was a mistake. He told me I had to give it to the company after I spilled my guts out and told him I was going to keep it, but I refused."

"You could've gotten a raise by turning it in," said Lily.

"Yes, I could've, but I wanted that nugget. It was probably the biggest piece of gold anybody has ever found. Your father told our boss about what I found and that I was refusing to turn it in. I ended up giving it to the company so I wouldn't get fired, but they fired me anyway that afternoon. That night I got drunk and angry because our boss gave your father the nugget I found, for his honesty and for being loyal over the years. Our boss told him never to give it away and to keep it, for one day it would be worth millions."

Deven turned to the fireplace and watched the fire for a second before turning back again.

"That night, when you were seven, I came looking for the nugget, but he hid it well. I had the idea to kidnap you so your father would give it to me, but he found his way out of that and told me to stay away from his family. I told him before I left that someday he would regret betraying me and I would get revenge on him and his family. Now, I have."

"What, by kidnapping me?" Lily yelled. "You have nothing to prove anymore, my father is gone. Make peace with yourself and leave me be."

"That was only part of my plan, Lillian. After my first plan failed."

Lily looked up at him with a worried look.

"What plan?"

"Well, you see, Lily, I killed your father and it was most refreshing to finally do it."

Lily was confused by his words and didn't want to believe what he had just told her. Lily felt a mix of shock, sadness, and disbelief all at once.

"The police said he died in his sleep," she said, confused as ever.

"Yes, that was the best part, no one suspected a murder. I slipped something in his drink and he was dead a minute later. Best thing about the poison is that it won't show up on the autopsy report. "

Lily couldn't believe what she just heard, she felt like her soul left her body. She looked down and started to tear up. Lily suddenly launched at Deven and started cursing.

"YOU MONSTER," Lily yelled at him. "HOW COULD YOU!"

He tripped backward and fell to the floor.

"Contain her, J.P.," he said to the man with different colored eyes.

He pulled and forced her to sit in the position she was just in. One of the men to her right came over to help him hold Lily still and the other man helped Deven up off the floor. Deven stared at Lily, he walked towards her and knelt to her level.

"My men told me you were a feisty pain in the ass, but now I gotta see it for myself."

He slapped her across the face and pulled her chin over so he could look at her in the eyes.

"You look like your mother, but those eyes are your father's eyes."

He stood back up and looked at Lily as he fixed his hair.

"Lily, you're going to be here for a while, so I wouldn't disrespect me again," Deven said to her in a harsh voice. "Now, tell me where the gold is hidden. I know you know where it is."

"I don't. He never told me where it was. I've never seen, nor heard of this gold until a few days ago."

"Fine. Have it your way. Take her back upstairs to my room and lock the door," Deven demanded.

J.P. took Lily by the arm and walked her out of the room.

"You can't do this Deven, let me go."

Lily tried hitting the man taking her back upstairs, hoping he would release her because of her strong punches. She was angry and sad, she had too many emotions going off inside her. The man pushed her into the room and then locked the door. Lily was left alone once again in the room. She stood up from off the floor and walked over to the fire poker to try and untie her wrists. Once her wrists were free, Lily rubbed them softly hoping to relieve some pain. Lily sat on the floor and cried a river thinking about what Deven had said. She knew that they were going to kill her eventually and she needed to find a way to escape.

  The man walked back downstairs and into the living room where Deven was still gazing intensely at the burning fire.

"Boss, I'm going into town to get some food and to see if they're looking for the brat. Jeff you come with me I need an extra pair of eyes," said J.P.

"Give me a second that little twit made me cut my arm last night, it needs a new bandage."

 Jeff wrapped his arm with a gauze bandage and pulled his sleeve back down.

 At the airport Janet and Owen had been circling the parking lot, searching for the BMW or the Mercedes. Owen parked the car around two in the morning, so they both could get some rest for their search the next day. At ten in the morning, Janet woke up smelling coffee and pastries. She glanced over and observed Owen devouring jelly-filled donuts as if he hadn't eaten in two days.

"Oh, I see you're finally awake. I bought us coffee and donuts."

"Thank You! So it's true about cops loving donuts, huh?" Janet laughed before she took a sip of her hot black coffee.

"I don't think that's entirely true, but donuts are one of my favorite breakfast foods," Owen chuckled.

He took another bite of the delicious deep-fried donut. The donut was so filled it bled jelly out the other end and ran down his hand.

"So, we know those men that took Lily are still here in Harpswell, but I have no clue where they could be hiding her. Is there anything that we've missed? Do you have any information that you and Lily haven't told me?" Janet listed things in her head and thought of everything she could.

"Well, we've told you what they look like, what they drive, and what they want. Did they ever find fingerprints on the paper?"

"No, they most likely used gloves," Owen replied.

"Did Lily tell you about the clues?"

"Yes, but she didn't mention much. Have you found any more clues."

"Yes, one in the library yesterday, and that led us to the lighthouse clue that was underneath the dock. Did Lily mention the secret room?"

"A secret room?"

"Yeah, behind the fireplace, that's where we found our first clue. The first clue was a note on the desk and was dated the day before he died. He wrote to Lily saying he left something behind for her, but she has to find it because someone is after whatever he left behind. These clues have led us everywhere around town, and I'm thinking these men are who he was warning us about."

Owen's eyes lit up from hearing all of this information.

"Why didn't this come up before? I could've protected you both or maybe helped you find these clues."

"I thought Lily had told you everything at the hospital. But, whatever her father left for her, I know for sure they want it. It's weird though, it almost feels like they planned this out."

They both tried to piece things together, and things were not adding up. "What I find weird is that the date on that letter you found was a day before he died," said Owen.

"Yeah. Oh my goodness!"

Lily's heart started to pump faster.

"What if someone was after her father for something, and to get back at him he's been after Lily? They said they wanted gold and they're probably using Lily to get it. But, she doesn't know where it is."

"Didn't her father work as a gold and silver miner?"

"Yes, he did. Maybe they worked with her dad and heard about Lily's father finding gold."

"That would make sense," said Owen.

Janet put pieces together in her head and thought of one possibility that she hoped wouldn't be true.

"Owen, what if they murdered Lily's father? I mean the man was forty-eight and Lily told me they don't have any heart problems in the family."

"I hate to think that might be a possibility, but there were no gunshot or stab wounds. Mr. Davis would have to be poisoned. We should do an autopsy to make sure. I'll call the office and tell them to do an autopsy on Mr. Davis today and we'll keep looking for Lily. If Mr. Davis was killed, then we need to find Lily before she ends up six feet under."

While Janet ate her donut and sipped her steaming hot coffee, Owen called James Cowell and talked to him about their situation. Owen told him to contact him when they got the results and to send men to continue searching for Lily.

"Ok, Officer Cowell said a pathologist would do an autopsy as soon as they can. Let's go ask around town if they've seen Lily or one of the cars last night."

"Sounds good. Hopefully someone was watching the streets last night, it might be our last hope to find her," Janet remarked.

Owen started the vehicle and pulled out of the airport parking lot. He drove past the library and downtown to park at the bank.

"Ok, let's find some clues," said Owen.

Janet looked at the Sergeant and could tell he was in love with Lily, it was so obvious. He wanted her safe and the look in his eyes assured Janet that he was the guy for her.

Owen and Janet start by asking people who lived next to the bank if they saw any of the two cars they described. One bad answer after another, Owen and Janet almost moved on from the area. They had one more house to ask across Tammie's Diner, before moving to a different area. They walked up the aged steps that led to the two-story house. The steps were covered with moss, making Janet search for the next step as she made her way up. Owen pushed the doorbell and a minute later an older woman opened her door with a smile and a 'how can I help you Sergeant?' Owen explained about the kidnapping the night before and asked if she saw a BMW or a black Mercedes.

"You know, I was sitting in my rocking chair around 6:30 or 7:00 and I did see a black BMW run the stop sign."

Janet looked at Owen with relief in her eyes, they had a small lead at last. "Do you remember which way they drove off? I mean, it is a four-way street," replied Owen.

"Yes, they continued going past my house."

"Thank you for that very important information, Miss. We'll be on our way. Have a great day."

Janet and Owen walked back down the stairs and to the car.

"This is a good lead. I have an idea where to go next," Owen said to Janet as he started the vehicle.

"Where are we going next?"

"Well, if they drove past her house that means they either kept driving straight or turned down another street. The only way to find out is the security cameras from the grocery store."

"Now we're getting somewhere, good thinking."

Owen and Janet were so focused on seeing the security footage that they didn't see the black Mercedes pull into the parking lot of the grocery store a couple of cars away from them. Jeff dropped off J.P. at the entrance and parked where he would be able to see him come back out.

When Janet and Owen walked in they asked an employee to see the manager. The employee walked him back to his office and the manager agreed to let them see the footage from last night. He led them into a room where six or seven TVs were sitting on two tables. Some of the TVs showed customers shopping and the other TVs showed the outside of the building.

Two security guards were sitting at the tables watching the footage and talking about things outside of work. The guards turned around when the manager, Janet, and Owen walked in.

"Carter, Sergeant Jackson would like to see the footage from around 6:30 last night on the north side of the building, please," the manager instructed. Janet watches the screen carefully as he zooms back the footage from the last few hours.

"The good thing, Sergeant, is that you came just in time. Our footage erases after 24 hours," Carter said. "Ok, here we go. At 6:30 pm, Tuesday, May 28th."

Owen and Janet leaned closer to the TV and watched the screen intently, looking for the BMW to drive by or the Mercedes. After watching for two minutes a black BMW drove by, speeding and continuing forward.

"Ok, we know they went straight now," Janet said with joy in her voice. "They must be heading out of town. Thank you so much for your help."

"No problem, happy to help."

Janet and Owen both smiled and celebrated when they walked out of the room. They were another step closer to finding Lily. When they turned the corner Janet's body froze like it was in shock. She saw J.P. twenty feet away about to leave the checkout.

"Owen! That's the man. The man with different colored eyes!"

Owen and Janet walked at a quick pace over to where J.P. was standing. J.P. saw them coming towards him, he grabbed his two bags and started to run for the doors. Janet and Owen chased after him, and Owen yelled at people to stop J.P. from going outside. J.P. pulled out a walkie-talkie from his pocket and told Jeff to bring the Mercedes to the entrance fast. He was slipping away from them, just a couple of feet away and Owen would be able to grab his jacket.

Owen and Janet were getting closer and closer, hope filled Janet's head that they would be able to reach J.P., but he was out the doors. He looked back to make sure Owen and Janet were not close enough to reach him. He looked back again and saw Owen and Janet coming out of the store, then he saw the Mercedes parked a couple of feet away. J.P. took his walkie-talkie out of his pocket to tell Jeff to unlock the Mercedes. When he took out his walkie-talkie his wallet slipped out and dropped to the ground. He jumped in the Mercedes and was almost out of sight by the time Janet and Owen were in the parking lot.

Owen kicked a rock and screamed, thinking they were so close to getting to Lily. Janet stopped running and took a deep breath next to Owen. Janet was furious and wanted to throw something.

"I'm going back to the car, we can't waste any time," said Janet.

"Ok, I'll be there in a second."

Janet walked back to the car and waited for Owen to join her. Owen was about to walk back to the car, but then saw a wallet on the sidewalk. He decided to pick it up and looked inside hoping to find an ID, and he did. But, it wasn't the ID he would ever suspect, it was J.P's wallet. Owen jogged back to the car and told Janet to get in.

"Why do you have a freaking smile on your face, Owen? We just lost the one man that could've led us to Lily."

"I know, but look what I found."

He tossed the wallet to Janet, and when Janet looked at the ID her face lit up like a thousand fireflies in July.

"This is his ID! How did you get this?"

"It was on the sidewalk! He must've dropped it running to his car."

"This is awesome. We can look this guy up and maybe find some information," said Janet.

"Yeah, let's head back to the station and find some files on Jason Parlo.

Chapter XVII

Drugs, Thorns, And A Bad Attitude

    Just as Owen pulled into the police station, they saw James Cowell walking out of the building. Janet noticed a disturbance in James's face as they walked up to the vehicle. Janet could tell something was wrong. Owen shut off the car and James waited for them to step out to talk to them.

"Hey, James! Do you have any leads?"

"No, no one found anything, but there is something you must know. Actually, something you both should know."

"Well, what is it?"

"Um, we found a large amount of thallium in Mr. Davis's body. It was in different parts of his nervous system. He wouldn't have been able to fight it if he wanted to."

Janet's heart dropped into her stomach and tears started to form in her eyes, blurring everything around her.

"Sir, we searched his house and couldn't find the drug anywhere."

Janet couldn't take in the news she heard from Office Cowell, so she went inside to Owen's office. Owen followed Janet up to his office and when he sat down in his chair he covered his face with his hands.

"Are you ok?" asked Janet.

"Yeah, just trying to piece this all together. How are we going to tell Lily her father was murdered?"

Owen pulled out the wallet from his pocket and grabbed the man's ID card.

"Took a few minutes to find his file, but here he is, thirty-two-year-old Jason Parlo from North Carolina. He was charged with aggravated robbery on December 8th, 1995. Jason was sentenced to sixty months in prison, which I believe is 5 years, and was released November 20th, 1990."

"Seven months ago," said Janet.

"He must've moved out here and found someone that had a grudge against Mr. Davis."

"So, we know he's a criminal and possibly committed murder, but we don't know who he's working for, how he got that drug, and where they took Lily."

"Well, we also know that they drove past the store and were heading out of town. We searched the airport, so they must be hiding her in a house. I'm going to see if we have a map of the town that we can mark houses we haven't checked."

Owen walked out of the room and Janet sat looking out the window. She found her eyes landing on the wallet and decided to look through it. "Looking another time couldn't hurt," Janet told herself.

Janet took all the cards and some receipts out of the wallet and started reading the receipts.

"Tammie's dinner, grocery store, and barber shop. Janet took a notepad off Owen's desk and wrote down the places he'd shopped at. She then read off the black ink on the printed cards.

"Credit card, Jack's pizza coupon, Quick Brew coupon, and what's this?" The last card had the business name called Fast Drugs, the owner's name, and the number. Janet stared at the card and knew that's where he got the drug to kill Lily's father. It all connected in Janet's head and she had an idea. Janet waited patiently for Owen to come back with the map which didn't matter anymore. After a few minutes, Owen came back into the room and placed the map down on his desk.

"Owen, I've been waiting for you, I found something in his wallet. We haven't looked at the cards yet and I found this card that I believe will be our ticket to find Lily."

Janet handed Owen the card and when he read it he had the biggest smile.

"Gotcha, so this is where he got a hold of the drug," Owen said to himself out loud.

"Yeah, and I have a plan!"

"Ok, let's hear it."

"Just let me say you might not agree to do this because of your job and it's illegal. I'm thinking you call that number on the card and play it off as if you know Jason. When you call asking for drugs, mention you're already in Maine and tell them you can meet them somewhere in town. I'll lay in the trunk and, when you make the exchange, I'll get out when he leaves. Then, we follow him and see where he goes."

"Janet, you're brilliant, that's a perfect plan. But, it's going to be risky and some of their men might recognize me."

"Thank you. Maybe I should become a cop, or maybe a bounty hunter." Owen laughed and then raised his eyebrows.

"You could, you have the wit and passion to do it. Ok, give me a fake name to use," Owen told Janet.

"Let's see…. How about Brian Higgins?"

"That works. Read me the number on the card and the owner's name."

"Deven Stonewall and the number is 207-882-5540."

Owen picked up the phone and dialed the number.

"Hello, is this Mr. Stonewall?" said Owen.

"Yes, who's asking? asked Deven.

"My name is Brian Higgins and my accomplice told me you might have some marijuana to sell me."

Owen looked at Janet and winked at her to show it was going as they planned.

"Yes, we have a large stock. A pound costs $2,000, so how much do you want?"

Owen looked at Janet and thought of an offer that Deven would like.

"Two pounds will do for now," Owen replied. "I am already in Harpswell, so could one of your men meet me somewhere in an hour?"

"That will be fine, but not in town. A man will meet you at the lake parking lot. He'll be driving a black Mercedes at eleven sharp, so do not be late."

"Perfect," said Owen.

Deven hung up and Owen looked back at Janet.

"We got him."

"Owen, I just thought of this. What if he sends J.P.? He knows what you look like."

"I'll have James join us and we'll fill him in on the plan. We can park my truck a few squares over and hide in the bushes until the exchange is over."

"Ok, yeah that works," said Janet.

"Well, we better get going, we have an hour to do this," Owen said as he walked out of his office.

Owen and Janet went downstairs and found a volunteer, James. Owen, James, and Janet drove to

Owen's House to get some backup clothes and supplies.

"So, this is where you live," said Janet.

"Yep, home sweet home. I'm just going to go grab a change of clothes for me and James and I'll be right back."

Owen left Janet outside by his truck who quickly became bored and thirsty. Janet wanted to go inside and get a drink,so and that's what she ended up doing. She walked into the house and looked around. There was a nice fireplace and two couches, and above the fireplace is a beautiful abstract oil painting. Hills rolling into mountains and flowers made it all pop with its vibrant bright colors. As Janet was drinking from the glass of ice water, Owen and James came down the stairs changing into some casual everyday clothing.

"You guys ready?"

She startled them since they thought they left her by the truck.

"Hey, good thing you came in here. Come into the living room," Owen told Janet. "Ok guys, listen up. After we locate the house or wherever they are keeping her, we find two ways to get in. James is going to have the dangerous part in this, sorry James. You're going to drive up to the house and pretend one of the bags has flour instead of marijuana, to try and stall for us."

"What? Are you nuts?" James snapped.

"Just let me finish. Janet and I are going to find a way to save Lily. And if we're not out by the time you're done distracting them, James, call the cops immediately. I already told one of the officers to stand by. Does this sound like a good plan?"

"Yeah. let's do it. Sounds good to me."

"Yeah, I'm in," said Janet.

"Here, you'll be needing these."

Owen handed Janet a larger knife to slide in her short brown boot then gave her a small pistol.

"You think you can shoot that?"

"Yeah, I can shoot," Janet replied as she shoved it in the back of her pants. Owen and James loaded up with their weapons and handcuffs. James's handcuffs had to be hidden in his jacket so he wouldn't get caught. James, Owen, and Janet jumped in the truck and drove into town. Janet and James both were watching out for the Mercedes on the road so they didn't screw up the plan. They were a minute away from the lake parking lot when they made a rapid decision to pull over on the side of the road.

"I don't want to take a chance. If he is in the parking lot already then the plan is wasted and we could get Lily killed by our actions. I'm thinking me and Janet get out here and you continue to the parking lot. We'll be somewhere in the bushes hiding."

"Ok, better safe than sorry," said James.

Owen and Janet jumped out of the truck and shut the door. Janet looked at James, who was now at the wheel.

"You'll do fine, James. We'll see ya in a few minutes."

He drove off with a worried look in his eyes, but he was brave and continued to the lake parking lot.

Janet and Owen jogged carefully off the road so they wouldn't be seen, and eventually arrived at the lake parking lot. The Mercedes and James were already there and the two men were talking. They were facing towards the lake chatting away and, when the men turned around Owen could see it was Jason Parlo talking to James. Owen slowly crawled closer to get a better look and then turned back at Janet.

"Janet, that's Jason."

"Well, good thing we had James come along. Why are they taking so long?"

"He's probably talking about the deal. I knew James could do this, James and I go way back. We both graduated from the same college and he was one of the best detectives I knew. He moved out here two years ago and I was offered a job as a Sergeant."

"Wow, I didn't know you both were that close and that he was once a detective."

"He's thinking about being a detective again."

"I think he should."

Janet could see the two men walking over to the back of the Mercedes. The trunk opened and he pulled a large suitcase out. He shook James's hand and James walked back to Owen's truck with the suitcase. Owen and Janet waited until the Mercedes pulled out to make their way over to the truck. When Owen and Janet got in the truck they congratulated James for playing it off so well and started the truck.

"You did so well! Now, let's follow our bait."

The Mercedes was heading out of town and Owen was not far behind him. He kept a good distance between them so they wouldn't be spotted. When they turned down a back road near the airport, the Mercedes was nowhere in sight.

"Where did he go?" asked Janet, scrunching her face.

"I don't know, it's like he disappeared out of thin air," Owen replied. "Well, this is a dead end, I'm going to turn around and check the houses."

They backtracked, looking for any sign of the vehicles or anything suspicious.

"Well, if J.P. turned down this road he is in one of these houses," James said confidently.

"Let's park the car up here at this house and let them know it's only temporary."

They parked the car, talked to the owners of the house, and started searching the few houses down the road. They had no luck when they searched the houses and they wondered if there was another road they didn't see or a house they missed. As they made their way back Janet saw black tire markings on the road where the road ended.

"Owen, come look at this. We might have something."

"What is it?"

"These tire marks continue into the woods."

Janet walked beside the bushes and looked down.

"OW!"

Janet had walked into a small growing hawthorn tree. The small thorn tree slit two holes in her leggings. Blood slowly came out of her small scrapes, but it wasn't anything to fuss about.

Janet continued on and when she was behind the bushes she saw a driveway. Just as she suspected.

Owen and James followed behind her and Owen's spirit was lifted knowing they had probably found her.

"A hidden road! Wait a minute. I believe this road used to lead to the mines," remarked James.

"Well, that makes more sense," Janet said to herself.

"What does?" asked Owen.

"Well, Lily's father worked for the mining company most of his life, the owner of the drug company must've worked in the mines with Mr. Davis."

"It's all connected. I think you could have something there," Owen said. "Nice work, Janet. Have you ever considered working in the criminal justice area?"

"I mean, a little. I used to pretend I was catching the bad guy, which was my brother, and I would tie his hands with the kitchen towel."

James put his hand on Janet and laughed, then followed Owen into the woods.

Janet stood there and small goosebumps formed on her arms. She was starting to like James. Just something about him makes him different from all the other guys she's dated. He laughed at her jokes and seems to always have this brave, positive energy.

She followed the two men through the woods and couldn't stop thinking about James. Janet had thought about James, but the feelings weren't as strong as they were now. Should she tell him her feelings? Janet wasn't sure, she needed to stay focused for now. The three walked through the woods following the road from a distance and eventually could see a house.

"After all this time searching, we finally found her," Owen said with excitement.

"Yep, we did it, but we still have to get her out," said Janet.

"This house looks old, but well kept up," remarked Janet.

"Yeah, they must've renovated the house when the mines went out. This house was abandoned years ago, at least that's what we thought," James told Janet.

"Ok, this is what we're going to do," Owen said, bringing them closer. "James, you're going to go back to the truck and replace two of the bags with the flour I hid under the seat. Then, drive up to the house and when we see that you are distracting them, Janet and I will sneak into the house through a window or back door."

"Sounds like a decent plan," remarked James. "How long do you need me to stall for?"

"At least fifteen to twenty minutes," replied Owen.

"If you don't see us by the driveway entry then, drive as fast as you can to the police station and call for help."

"You got it, boss."

"Ok, let's get her out, and be safe, James. Don't get yourself killed."

Janet took her time hugging him and told him good luck. She looked back at James as he jogged back to the truck that was still parked at the stranger's house. She walked low through the bushy woods and crouched down by Owen. But, when her hand hit the ground she was pricked by a thorn bush that was right next to her.

"OUCH! I did it again! These damn thorns keep stabbing me."

"Well, you'll have to be more careful and quiet, we're almost right next to the house."

They waited for James to drive up to the house, so they could make their move. It was around one in the afternoon, and the sun broke through the trees, lighting up the woods for Janet and Owen to see the crunchy leaves on the ground. They needed to be quiet to sneak to the side of the house. Owen suddenly stops and quickly puts his hand on Janet and they both drop to the ground. He slowly gets up, looks around after a couple of seconds, and then crouches back down.

"I spotted our way into the house," Owen said to Janet with a huge smirk on his face.

"Where?"

"There's a cracked open window on the left side of the house. Do you see it?"

Janet took a look at the window and thought it was a perfect way to get in. Owen watched the house like a hawk, while Janet looked for James to drive down the driveway.

"I wonder if James chickened out," Owen jokingly said to Janet, as he waited and waited for action.

Janet finally could hear James coming down the driveway and nudged Owen.

"I hear him. He's coming."

"Ok, any time now that front door will open."

And he was right, the door opened and two men stepped out of the house to greet James. The two men looked familiar to Janet. She looked closer and realized they were the two goons that were chasing Lily around the library.

They walked up to the truck and started talking to James. Janet could tell he was explaining his visit by seeing his hand movements. He was telling a convincing story and played it off well because one of the men started to lead him into the house. The other man grabbed the box and followed them inside. He shut the door and that was Janet and Owen's cue to sneak inside.

"Ok Janet, this could be dangerous. These men want to kill both of you and will want to kill both me and James. I should make you stay here, but I need your help, as well. Keep watch for me and stay a few feet back from me, because if one of us gets caught the other can still get Lily. This is a big house, so try to find a darker place to hide by, and don't get yourself killed."

"Hey, we can do this. We just need to watch each other's backs and get her out fast. I'm thinking she's upstairs," Janet remarked.

"Then let's check upstairs first."

Owen had his handgun ready in his hand and ran low to the window. Janet waited for Owen to signal her over, and when he did she ran low just as he did.

"Take out your knife and be ready for anything," Owen said in a hushed voice.

Janet did as he said and took her pocket knife out of her right boot. Owen peaked in the window and then started to push the window open. The gap became bigger as he pushed it open and, when it was large enough to fit through, he took off his backpack and slid inside. Janet handed Owen his backpack and then joined him. Owen helped her up and then closed the window to where it was before.

   Janet looks around the hallway and waits for Owen. She could hear men talking somewhere in the house. Their voices echoed through the house as if they were in a cave, and sent chills through Janet. She felt as if she was in a war zone, hiding from their enemies. Owen put his finger over his lips telling Janet to keep at a quiet pace, as they made their way through the house. The hardwood floor was repaired and stained, it was nice looking but it also made it easier to walk around without any creaks and squeaking. Janet could hear James's voice down the hall, talking business to the men and Mr. Stonewall. Owen and Janet quietly walked down the hallway, hoping to not be seen while checking every room.

"Owen, someone's coming!" She whispered.

   He opened the door next to them and hid behind a chair with Janet. The room was still. Nothing moved but shadows walking past the door. They stayed as quiet as possible so they wouldn't get caught and ruin the whole plan. Janet looked over to a white tarp hiding a stack of boxes next to her. Curiosity made Janet peak at the labels on the side of the box.

   The boxes were filled with bottles of chloroform, and that gave her an idea. Janet tugged on Owen's shirt and pointed to the boxes.

"What if we knock Deven's men out? This would be easier without active madmen trying to kill us."

Owen looked at the label on the box and thought it was a good idea, as well. Janet cut the cloth tarp with her knife and soaked the cloth with chloroform.

Owen takes the cloth from Janet and waits behind the door. He stomps on the ground with his left foot, hoping the man will hear it and come into the room. He hears nothing and decides to stomp louder. Owen and Janet could hear someone coming towards the door and got ready. Janet stayed hidden behind the crates and waited for the man to walk in. The door opened and Janet could see the man checking the room. He walked forward and, before he turned around, Owen came up behind him knocking him out with the soaked cloth.

Owen drops him slowly to the floor and tells Janet to open the closet door. He drags the young man into the walk-in closet and strips him of all his weapons. Owen shuts the closet door and places a chair under the door handle.

"He won't be bothering us."

Janet looked back at Owen and laughed, then took her gun out.

"Ladies first," Janet told Owen.

"Haha, you're so funny. Get behind me."

Owen looked before going out and then checked the stairs. Owen backed up and told Janet to hide in the corner behind an armchair. A man comes down the stairs and walks towards the front door. Owen held his gun up beside his face and checked if it was clear for them to go upstairs. Janet watched Owen and waited for a signal. Then, something caught her eye.

She stayed as still as possible. It was too late to warn Owen. Someone was behind him. She could see the man's dark shadow sneaking up on Owen, then she could see his body. He didn't see Janet hiding behind the armchair because his eyes were locked on the back of Owens' head. Owen was screwed and Janet couldn't do or say anything.

Before Owen continued, he heard a click. Owen stopped immediately, he knew what it was, and then he felt it. A gun barrel was pointed at the back of Owen's head, he couldn't move, and he was caught.

"Nice to see you, Sergeant Jackson."

Chapter XVIII
Bad News, Headaches, and Another Plan

Owen raised his hands in the air and prayed that Janet wasn't seen.

"Put the gun on the floor and turn around, Jackson."

Owen did as he said and faced J.P. Owen looked him in the eyes and could tell J.P. was overjoyed to have Owen where he wanted him.

"Looking for your girlfriend, I assume?"

"Where is she, you jackass?"

"I have a better question. Where's the other girl? I know she's here somewhere. I saw you both on the cams outside. Tell me where she is and I might not kill you."

"You don't scare me, Parlo. She's probably calling the rest of the station as we speak. You, your buddies, and your boss will be sentenced to life in prison, I'll make sure of it. The last time you were in prison was just a taste of hell, this time it will be your home."

"One last chance Jackson, where is the girl?"

Owen kept staring at J.P. with his hands still above his head. J.P. came at Owen and pushed him against the wall. Owen looked at the armchair and could see Janet was still hidden, she was small enough not to be found. J.P. patted Owen and stripped him from all his weapons. He put Owen's extra bullets on the floor, along with his knife and second gun. He then pointed his gun at Owen's back and gripped the right side of his neck.

"Come on sarge, let's take a walk."

Janet heard J.P. walk off with Owen and decided to stand back up. She waited until they were totally out of sight to make a run up the stairs. Janet prayed for Owen and asked God to keep them both alive a little longer for her to save them. Janet runs up the stairs and starts checking the rooms. She listens for any voices before opening the doors and then closing them again.

Lily wasn't in any of the rooms that she had checked so far, and she was starting to doubt they kept her upstairs. Janet opened the last door and shut it behind her. She spots Lily's dress draped over the end of the bed. This is where they've been keeping Lily. But where is she?

Janet runs around the room looking for Lily. She checked the closet, the bathroom, on the couch, but she wasn't in the room. She looked over to her left and saw bottles on the nightstand, and ropes lying on the bed. Janet walked over to the nightstand and looked closer at the bottles. When she read the labels she was disgusted, and horrified. Tears trickled down her cheeks and wet her lips. They were injecting her with zolpidem. Too much of this drug could make anyone go insane.

Janet sat on the bed and wiped her tears with her jacket sleeve. Too many ideas popped into her head of what happened to Lily in this room. Janet took a deep breath and forced herself to stop crying. If Lily wasn't upstairs they must have her somewhere downstairs, probably where they took Owen. How to get them both out without getting caught or killed would be a challenge. A challenge Janet didn't know if she could pull off, but what choice did she have?

Janet needed to think fast. What could she do to save them both? She stood up and looked around the room for anything she could use. Of course there wasn't a phone in the room, but she could probably find one downstairs. She looked over to the door and saw Owen's backpack lying on the floor and wondered what was in his book bag. She never asked what he put in the bag, but was lucky enough to end up with it.

Janet rushed over to the bag and opened the top. She looked inside and started pulling out items he packed. She first pulled out a first aid kit and a bag of extra bullets. Then her eyes lit up as if she saw a check for half a million dollars. A phone! Something she could use at the moment. Janet dialed the police station and waited for someone to pick up on the other side.

"Hello!"

"Harpswell Maine Police Department, what is your emergency?"

"Yes, the sergeant and I went looking for my friend who was kidnapped, the chief already has heard about it. Sergeant Jackson is in trouble and he needs backup right away!"

"Ok, miss what is your location?"

"I'm not sure, but Owen told the cops where we were. We are a few miles out in the country in the old mine house. The driveway is hidden from the road, but you can spot it easily by seeing the swerved tire marks."

"Ok miss, I'm going to send officers over there immediately. Stay where you are. Help will be there in a few minutes," said the woman.

"Perfect, thank you!"

Janet hung up and put the phone on the floor next to her. She continued taking things out of the bag, checking for anything she could use. At the bottom of it, she pulled out a bag of flour. Janet laughed and then questioned why he had a bag of flour in his backpack. She looked at the other equipment in the bag, a few handcuffs, wire ties, and batteries for the flashlight. She tried thinking of a good plan because if anything happened in a few minutes, they both could be dead.

Janet looked at the equipment again and suddenly she had a crazy idea. She told herself 'no, the plan she had in mind was too risky and could most likely get her killed.' But, her gut told her to do it, since it was the only plan she could think of. In her mind, she planned out what was going to happen. First, she needed to gather everything and put it in Owen's backpack. Janet grabbed all the handcuffs, wire ties, and flour, then shoved the bag of extra bullets in her jacket.

While Janet was looking at the drug bottles and thinking of an insane idea, Owen was being pushed and shoved down a hallway. He looked at the doors on his left and on his right. He didn't know what door he would be going into. His heart was beating rapidly. He started to feel the sweat on his forehead slowly drip down the side of his face. He had an unsteady mind and rubbed his thumb up and down his sweaty palms. Owen's eyes were focused on the doors in front of him, but then J.P. told Owen to stop walking.

When Owen stopped he knew it was the perfect time to fight back. When J.P. tried reaching for the doorknob Owen grabbed his arm, threw him against the wall, and punched him repeatedly in the gut. Owen was about to knock J.P. out, when two men came out of the room they were about to enter and pointed their guns directly at Owen's head. He screwed up and couldn't get out of this. He might've just made it worse for himself, but it was definitely worth it.

Owen had no choice but to put his hands up and stay absolutely still. Jason stood up and took a second to breathe before punching Owen in the stomach.

"How do you like the taste of your own medicine, sarge? Doesn't feel great, does it? Take him inside," ordered J.P.

The two men grabbed Owen, pulled him up, and forced him through the door. When Owen entered the room he saw something unexpected, someone he couldn't wait to see. It was Lily.

He wanted to break down in tears seeing her duck taped to a chair, surrounded by the men who had destroyed her mentally and physically. Lily was no longer wearing her long flowing green dress. She was wearing almost nothing, just a bra and black shorts. He could see the bruises on her face, legs, and arms, and it tore him up inside. Lily's lower lip was cut and bloody, and so was the cut on her right cheekbone. He could see she had been drugged with something. She looked drained and pale.

When Lily realized Owen was in the room she tried to say something, but it was a mumbled mess from the duct tape over her mouth. Owen saw James in the corner of the room sitting at a table with two other men, one of them being Deven. He tried to ignore James so he wouldn't blow his cover, but from a quick look at James, Owen could tell he was concerned. Owen sped over to Deven with anger trying to knock him out, but his men pulled Owen back before he got to do it. Deven stood up and walked over to Owen and looked him in the eyes.

"So, you're Sergeant Jackson. I've heard you've been a pain in the ass, tracking me down, chasing my best man in the parking lot. Big mistake trying to save Lillian."

"It's my job, and I promised her I would find her and kick your ass."

"Oh, I get it. You love her, am I right?"

Owen refused to respond. Giving him any information could make it worse for him and Lily.

"Let's talk, shall we? Boys give him a chair." ordered Deven.

One of the men sitting at the table stood up and placed a chair in front of Deven. Two men forced Owen into the chair and tied his hands and ankles down. Deven walked over to Lily, ripped the tape off her mouth, and grabbed a chair to sit in front of her.

"Now that we have the sergeant here, maybe you'll talk now my dear."

Lily wouldn't look at Deven and that made him angry.

"I'm not telling you anything, because I don't know where it is," Lily said.

Deven was becoming impatient and furious with Lily, but he had a plan that might change her mind. He stood up and walked over to the table. Deven picked up a black slender tank and placed it beside Owen. A younger man attached a tube to the tank and at the other end of the tube was a mask. Owen and Lily both watch the man and start to get very nervous, especially Owen.

"Ok, this is what's going to happen. You're going to give me a valid answer when I ask, and if you don't Mr. Jackson will breathe in nitrogen from that mask that Jason is holding."

"You are a sorry excuse for a man," Lily said to Deven.

"My dear Lillian, didn't your father ever teach you to respect your elders."

Owen could see the worry on James's face as he stood watching with another man by the door. He couldn't do anything because he was outnumbered, and would just make things worse for him and both Lily and Owen. It pained him to just stand and watch as they torched his best friend and beat Lily to death. The feeling of watching them was horrific, like he was stuck in a horror movie.

Deven slapped Lily across the face from the remark she had just made. Owen tried breaking loose from his chair, but was unable to because of the tight duck tape.

"You loathsome son of a bitch!" Owen yelled at Deven.

Deven looked over at J.P. and nodded. Owen looked back at J.P. and saw the mask coming towards his face. He tried pulling away, but it was too late. It was pressed over his mouth and nose. He couldn't breathe. Two seconds in and he was suffocating. Lily yelled at J.P. telling him to stop, but he continued suffocating him with the nitrogen. Deven lifted his hand telling J.P. to take it off Owen's face. When Jason released the mask, Owen breathed hard. His head was spinning from the few seconds of the nitrogen, his vision was slightly blurry when he looked down, and he was tired from fighting it.

"Ok, now that you've seen him in pain, do you have anything to tell me, my dear?"

Lily looked over to Owen, he was breathing hard looking down at his lap. She couldn't tell him what she knew, but she couldn't let Deven kill Owen. She needed a miracle to happen and needed it to happen quickly. Good thing Janet had a plan.

Janet was almost ready to go, she just needed to check her gun. She put Owen's backpack on, grabbed her gun, and opened the door slowly. Looking around in the hallway she saw nothing, no one in sight. Janet walked quickly down the hallway and looked down the stairs checking for any men.

The timing was perfect, she had just a few minutes before the cops would be at the house. Janet did not know what was going on downstairs, but knew she needed to get to them quickly. She had to accept that her plan could go sideways, but needed to stay positive that it would work. Every second counted.

Janet rushed down the stairs with light feet after checking if it was clear. She then walked slowly down the hallway, the one that J.P. had taken Owen down. Janet pressed her ear against the doors listening for any voices. The first three doors were silent, then she heard a scream from one of the rooms down the hall. Janet could tell it was Owen screaming in pain.

Janet rushed to the end of the hallway and heard people talking in the last room on the right. She took Owen's backpack off and placed it quietly on the floor. When Janet opened the bag she took out the flour, handcuffs, and wire ties. She was ready to go in, but Janet stopped herself before she barged into the room. She didn't know if she could pull it off. Her plan could fail and they would all be screwed. She should wait for the police…. but every second counted.

Janet took a deep breath and decided she was going to do what she planned. She opened the packet of flour and got ready. She then opened the door and quickly looked where everyone was. She held up the flour and shook it all over the room. The flour slowly started to fill the room with powdery "smoke", making it harder to see. Janet's presence caught everyone off guard.

James understood the assignment as soon as he saw Janet barge into the room. He started throwing punches, and knocked out the two men he was standing beside. Janet could hear the men drop to the floor, and when the flour ran out she ran to the men on the floor and zip-tied their hands together.

"Janet! Thank God you're here," Lily told Janet with excitement and relief.

"It was a team effort finding you, girl!"

Janet could slightly see James fighting Jason and Deven making it out the door. Janet acted quickly, took out her gun and chased after him. Deven could feel her presence and shot his gun at Janet while he was running. Thinking he shot her he slowed down, but heard steps continuing behind him. Janet shot her gun back at Deven. Bullets were flying past him, hitting the walls. After James had knocked out J.P. and put him in handcuffs, he realized Janet and Deven were missing. He quickly cut Owen's hand loose and gave him the knife to free himself and cut Lily loose.

James took out his gun and ran out the door to chase down Deven and Janet. Janet continued to run after Deven, but slowed down to avoid the bullets that missed her body by a few inches. He cowardly ran out the back door, firing back at Janet like a madman. Deven stood at the edge of the woods pointing his gun at Janet.

"It's over Deven. Your men are in cuffs and the cops are on their way," Janet said in a confident voice.

Deven smiled back at Janet's choice of words, and that made her wonder. A second later she heard a click and knew what it was. Another one of Deven's men was pointing a gun at Janet's neck. How did she forget about the man who walked down the stairs earlier?

"Put your gun down," Deven told Janet as he came closer.

Janet had no choice, she dropped her gun and raised her hands in the air. He grabbed her gun off the ground and checked her for any more weapons. He had found her extra bullets and a backup knife and put them in his pocket. Deven then fled into the woods with Janet in his clutches. James rushed outside and back into the house. "Where are they?"

He looked out the window and saw cop cars and an ambulance pull into the driveway.

"Janet, you are impressive," James said to himself.

He rushed outside and greeted the cops who rushed out of their cars. "Sergeant Jackson and a hostage are in the last room in the left hallway. Have a few men come with me. I think the boss of this operation is in the woods with a woman. She might be in trouble."

Four cops followed James around the house and into the woods. Cops rushed into the house to arrest the men and take Lily and Owen to the ambulance. Lily and Owen were relieved to see the cops take the men away. Owen sat on the floor and fell back with his eyes closed resting, with Lily lying next to him. They both had bruised ribs and deep cuts. Lily was exhausted and Owen was barely awake. A man and woman checked Lily and Owen then lifted them onto stretchers. Owen moaned from the pain of movement. They took Lily and Owen into the ambulance and drove to the hospital. The cops continued patting down the men and took them outside to read them their rights.

Deven stopped and gave the other man the zip tie he took from Janet's jacket pocket. He tied her wrists together and pushed her down to the ground.

"You might have saved Lillian and the sarge, but you have no hope of rescue," Deven said confidently.

"You see, I was going to shoot you but that would give away our location. We'll have to do this the messy way."

Janet tried to get up, but was kicked in the stomach by the man standing over her. She looked up and watched as Deven came closer with her own knife they had just taken from her boot. She thought that her life was soon to be over, but caught a glimpse of hope behind Deven.

"Drop that knife and put your hands in the air," James yelled to Deven. They were surrounded by all five cops and Deven had no choice but to obey.

He and the man standing beside Janet did as they were told. Janet was relieved, it was over. The men stripped their weapons from their possessions and cuffed them both. James ran over to Janet and cut the zip tie that was holding her wrists together. When Janet was free she wrapped her arms around him and didn't let go.

"Thank you, James. You saved my life, a minute more and I would've been dead. Are Owen and Lily safe?"

"Yes, they just reported on the radio that they're on their way to the hospital."

"Will you drive us to the hospital? I want to be with Owen and Lily."

"Yeah, let's get out of here," replied James.

James helped Janet off the ground and looked over at Deven.

"You think this is over? You haven't seen the last of me. I'll be back."

Janet ignored his worthless remarks and continued walking. It was a long walk back to the truck, and Janet's cramps felt stronger as they continued. When they arrived at the house, Janet could see police everywhere, checking in the house, the outside areas, and questioning the men.

J.P. Glared hard at Janet, she looked away to avoid the memories of the terrible last few days. James started the car, pulled out of the woods, and onto the road. They would be at the hospital in fifteen minutes

Chapter XIX

Is That Jello?

   Janet sat in the truck looking out the window, staring at the never-ending pavement. The truck was too warm for Janet's liking and she decided to take her jacket off. She could see James looking over at her from the corner of her eye as she took off her jacket. Janet pretended like she didn't see him glance over, and threw her jacket in the backseat.

"You did well in there. I don't think I could go undercover like that," said Janet.

"Are you kidding me? You were amazing and so brave. You took out those men with flour and risked your life to chase down a criminal. You didn't just save Lily and Owen, you saved my life as well. Thank you."

"You're welcome. I'd be lying if I said I wasn't scared the whole time."

"I'm glad you're ok. You had me worried for a little bit. When I saw Owen come into that room I had no words. Then I didn't see you walk in and I didn't know what to think. I didn't know if you had been hurt, killed, or if you got away."

"Well, thank you for worrying about me. I was hoping you were ok. I thought they would make you do something or hurt Lily."

"No, I kept them on different subjects, so that wouldn't happen. But hey, I was wondering, if Owen and Lily still go on that date maybe you would want to go with me? We could make it a double date," James said in a quick voice.

 Janet felt her cheeks rise in a smile and knew she was probably blushing.

"Yeah, that sounds like fun. I have a question," said Janet. "You can tell that I like you can't you?"

"Yes, but I have had a crush on you since you answered that call in Hawaii. Then, your eyes caught me when I first saw you. They're such a beautiful shade of green."

"Thank you, that's so sweet James. Do you know what movies are playing?"

"I have no clue, but we'll talk to them and see if they still want to go. We might just have to go by ourselves. I don't know how long they'll be in the hospital for."

James pulled into the front parking lot and grabbed his badge.

"Ok, let's head inside," James said to Janet as they pulled up.

Janet and James rushed into the hospital and headed towards the front desk. The woman at the front desk was the same woman who helped Lily and Janet the last time they were there. Janet and James walked up to the desk and asked to have Lily and Owen's room numbers so they could see them right away.

"They're both in room 217," said the young woman.

James and Janet walked over to the elevator and waited for it to open. He pressed the second-floor button and waited to go up.

"it's great that they're both in the same room. I hope they're both alright," said Janet.

"I don't know, I hope so. Lily didn't look too good and Owen took in a lot of Nitrogen."

"Nitrogen!"

"Yeah, it was brutal having to watch. Deven will pay for what he has done."

"Yes, they all will."

They stepped off the elevator and saw Lily and Owen's door across the hall to the left. Janet was almost scared to go inside. She walked in slowly and felt her heart beating fast. Janet didn't want to see the damage done to Lily, but she needed to stand by her friend. Lily was still, sound asleep like sleeping beauty, but in a blue hospital gown. Her lower lip was cleaner than before but the bruises looked painful. The bruise on her arm had formed a pink-purple color not far off from turning black. James stood beside Janet and was sick to see what they had done.

A nurse opened the door and walked into the room. Janet watched as she put supplies in a cupboard, and then asked the woman to talk to her in the hallway.

"James," Owen called out from the other side of the room.

"Hey boss man, how are you feeling? I'm surprised you're awake. You took in a lot of nitrogen."

James walked over to Owen's bed and pulled up a chair next to him. Owen wore an oxygen mask and was dressed the same as Lily was.

"A little sore. I think I passed out in the ambulance. My head feels heavy from that nitrogen, and I think I broke a rib or two."

James walked over to the end of the bed where a clipboard hung and read the paper attached to it.

"Actually, you have three broken ribs, and it looks like they hooked you up on oxygen for a few days."

"Well, it feels like I broke everything. How's Lily doing?"

"She's sleeping right now and it looks like she is bruised everywhere. Janet's out talking to the nurse to get information. Hey, when you and Lily get out of here, you want to go on a double date?"

Owen chuckled, but stopped from the pain.

"Did you ask Janet on a date?"

"Yep!" James said with a smile.

"Congratulations man, that's awesome! I could tell you liked her. But, yeah, that would be fun. might be a while though."

Janet came back into the room and shut the door quietly, so Lily could stay sleeping.

"So, I don't know if you guys know this, but Deven gave her a good amount of drugs. They prescribed her flumazenil for a couple of weeks to help so I'll have to watch her carefully," Janet said to the boys.

"How bad is she?" asked Owen.

"A small bottle was empty on the dresser beside her bed, so I'm guessing it was a good amount. The nurse said she should be fine if she takes those pills and stays here for a few days. But, she has some large cuts and her whole body is bruised."

"Well, she will need all our support. Did you guys arrest them all?" Owen asked.

"Yes, they took them down to the station and are clearing the house right now. But I'm going to go home, change, and come back. And try and get some sleep Owen, she'll wake up soon."

"I will. Be safe," Owen replied.

"I'll go with you," James said.

"Aw, thanks Jame. Owen we'll see you in a bit."

They both left the room and took the elevator down to the first floor. Janet saw they were selling coffee in the lobby and had to buy a cup since she hadn't had coffee since that morning. Janet dragged

James over to the coffee stand and then headed out the hospital doors jaunty with her cup of coffee. James drove to Lily's father's house and talked about how much they had in common. Janet could tell she was blushing when he talked to her, she felt like a schoolgirl all over again.

Janet changed into something more comfortable when she arrived back at the house. She put on shorts and a t-shirt, and grabbed a bag to pack some things. She grabbed a picture frame of Lily's family, a blanket, and a pair of comfortable clothes for when she got out of the hospital. Janet zipped the bag and walked out the front door.

"Are you all set?" James asked.

"Yep, I grabbed some stuff for Lily, as well."

"Good. I was going to swing by Owen's house and grab his things, then head to my house. I also wanted to spend the night."

"Oh good, I'll have someone to talk to. Hey, you want to get some pizza before we settle at the hospital?"

"Yes, I'm starving and hospital food doesn't sound good at the moment." Janet laughed.

"Yeah, I don't want that either. I'm craving something hot and yummy. I'll go to my house first, it's closer than Owen's."

Janet sat in the truck and waited for James to be done with packing both his and Owen's bags. Her stomach was growling. She closed her eyes and pictured a platter of bread sticks with cheese sauce and a large pepperoni pizza. Her vision was interrupted by the truck door slamming. It was finally time to feed her stomach.

James drove into town and parked the truck in the back parking lot of the restaurant. Janet jumped out of the truck excited and ready to eat. James and Janet walked in, sat at a table, and agreed on a supreme pizza to split. James ordered an extra order of breadsticks and sauce because they scarfed down the other order. They both enjoyed each other's company and snacked on the other order of breadsticks. When the waiter set the pizza on the table Janet's eyes lit up.

"That looks great! I wish Owen and Lily could be here, Lily loves pizza."

"Well, that can be the first thing we all do together. We'll get a large pizza."

Janet grabbed a piece of pizza and cut into it immediately.

"Ouch! This is super hot," Janet said out loud.

"Well yeah, silly, it just came out!"

   The homemade pizza was thick and hearty. When she took a bite she could taste the warm, heavily loaded toppings melted into the cheese. The crispy thin-crust pizza was made to perfection and they almost finished the whole thing. James and Janet sat for a few minutes, letting their food settle before getting up to pay the check. James paid for their meal while Janet used the restroom, then waited for her in the parking lot.

"Thank you, James. That was delicious."

"You're welcome."

"Hey, can we make one last stop before we go back?" Janet asked

"Yeah, where do you want to go?"

"The flower shop. I wanted to talk with Jessie and get them some flowers."

"Yeah, sure. I'll park in the front right here. You want me to go in with you?" asked James.

"No. It should only take a few minutes. I'll be right back."

Janet picked out flowers and chatted with Jessie for a few minutes. James started to get worried and was about to go into the store, but saw Janet push open the door with her back, holding two vases of flowers. James stepped out of the truck and helped her.

"What were you girls talking about?"

"Oh, nothing much, just telling her how Owen and Lily are doing and that Owen was awake."

Janet smelled the flowers that were being held in between her thighs and looked back at James.

"Well, I know what flowers Lily likes. Believe it or not, Lily loves lilies. And I decided to get Owen a mixed variety."

"They smell amazing. I can smell them from where I'm at."

"They must be freshly picked," Janet replied.

They pulled into the hospital and parked. James threw all three book bags onto his shoulders and Janet carried both vases. A man opened the door for James and Janet and told them to have a good night.

"Thank you!" said Janet.

They took the same elevator and when they opened their door, Lily was awake talking to Owen.

"There she is!"

"Those are for me? Thank you!" Lily said with a smile.

Janet placed it down on the nightstand next to her and took a flower out of the vase for her to smell.

"I love the smell of lilies!" Lily said, smelling them.

"And Owen these are for you," Janet said.

She walked over to his bed and put them on the nightstand.

"Thank you Janet. We both needed a little color in this room."

"We also grabbed you some clothes for when you get out of here. We're both staying the night with you guys."

Janet looked at Owen from across the room and decided it was the best time to tell Lily about her father. The room felt dark when she told Lily how they found out her father had been murdered just days ago. But Lily told Janet she had already been told this information from Deven. Janet comforted her with a hug and gave her a tissue for her running tears. They talked until the nurse came in the room to give Lily her pills. The nurse told Janet when she needed to take them and asked to keep an eye on her.

Lily was told she could leave in two days if she felt alright, and that Owen would go home in two days, as well.

"It will take a good six weeks for your ribs to heal, so I would sit or lay down and stay away from doing activities or anything that will be painful."

"Well, that's good news. You both will be sore, but I'll take care of you both. Owen, you can stay with us until you heal," Janet suggested.

"I don't want to be a bother."

"No, you'll stay with us and I'll help you both."

"Alright, I'll stay. Thank you."

"Lily, I'll call our employees and tell them we'll be gone for six more weeks."

"Ok. Hey, is there a dinner menu around here, I'm starving?" Lily said to Janet.

"Yeah, when the nurse came in she put a clipboard on the nightstand."

Janet grabbed Both the clipboards and started to read the menu to Lily and Owen.

"Ok, we have two different meals. Either salisbury steak, mixed fruit, and chocolate cake, or mac n' cheese, salad, and green jello with fruit."

Lily's eyes widened. "Did you say JELLO? I love jello! I'll take that one."

"I'll take the other one," Owen said from across the room.

"Ok, I'll go down and get them. You want to come with me, James?"

"Yeah, I'll help you."

James and Janet took the elevator down to the first floor and looked at the map of the hospital that was on the wall.

"Ok, we need to go…. this way," Janet pointed her finger.

They made their way down the hallway and opened the cafeteria doors. It wasn't too busy considering it was eight-thirty. Decor hung from the ceiling, making the cafeteria more cheerful and bright. Janet and James stood behind a family and waited to grab Owen and Lily's meals.

The lunch ladies asked which meal they would like and handed them a tray. At the end, there was a spread of cookies, pieces of pie, and cake. Janet grabbed a piece of blueberry pie and placed it on Lily's tray. James was entranced by a huge monster cookie. He put it on Owen's tray and took one to eat on the way up to the room.

"Couldn't resist, huh?"

"Oh, that was probably the best monster cookie I've ever had."

James licked his lips repeatedly, tasting the flavor of the freshly baked cookie. Owen and Lily were happy to see Janet and James back in the room and they could finally eat.

"YES, JELLO!" Lily said excitedly.

"Yep, and I got myself some pie."

"That looks good. too. I'm so hungry right now. This jello tastes amazing. I haven't eaten anything in a while, I actually don't remember the last time I ate."

"Well, if you want anything else you let me know."

Lily scarfed down all her food, eating as if she hadn't eaten in weeks. Owen and Lily finished their meals and gave Janet their trays to take back to the cafeteria. Lily requested some cookies for later and apple juice to wash it down.

When Janet came back from the cafeteria, she chatted with Lily close to midnight and snacked on the pile of cookies. Lily told Janet everything that happened when she was kidnapped, memories from childhood with her parents, and how scared she had been these last few days. It was a long conversation from tears to giggles, but it eventually had to end. Janet slipped into her pajama pants and switched her shirt, then pushed the nurse assistance button for an extra blanket. It took a minute for a nurse to come, but Janet got her blanket and draped it over James.

The sun shone through the hospital windows, waking everybody up from their deep sleep. Janet rubbed her eyes and forced herself to stand up.

"Morning, everybody," Janet said jaunty. "Do you feel better now that you finally got to sleep?"

"No, my head hurts and I feel like throwing up. I can feel the bruises, but I feel good enough to leave today. I just need to take my pills. Owen, are you feeling alright?"

"Yeah, just don't feel like moving."

"Well, I talked to the nurse when you all went to bed and she said we can actually leave this afternoon, so you can chill in bed until then," Janet said.

"Here's the menu for breakfast. I'm getting dressed and then James and I will go get us all breakfast."

Janet looked over at James and realized he was still sleeping in the chair beside Owen's bed. Janet tiptoed behind James's chair and scared him awake yelling, "JAMES."

He jumped up and pressed his hand over his heart.

"Gosh Janet, you scared the soul out of me."

"Sorry. Actually, I'm not sorry, that was funny! I'm going to get dressed, you want to come with me to get breakfast?"

"Yeah, I'll come with you," James said while yawning.

They all decided on blueberry muffins, and when Janet and James came back upstairs Lily was out of bed staring out the window. Janet was glad she decided to get out of bed and move around a little. She was also shocked to see Lily not hurting too much knowing she was bruised everywhere. Her bruises were clearly visible, but Janet could only imagine what she really felt like inside.

   Lily sat back down in her bed and ate her breakfast with everyone else. She could tell that the muffins were not exactly fresh when she bit into it. They tasted old and stale, but her hunger was large and she couldn't ignore the angry growl of her stomach anymore that morning. The others agreed that the batch was bad and tasteless. Janet stood up and told everyone to put their muffins back on the tray and asked James for the truck keys.

   Janet left the hospital and came back twenty minutes later with a box of donuts.

"Did you run to the store? You didn't have to do that," Owen said.

"Well, those muffins were disgusting and James still looks tired, so this should wake you all up."

"OH, long Johns are the best!" Owen said as he grabbed one from the box.

   The room was quiet after everyone grabbed their donuts. After they finished, Lily saw Jello on the breakfast menu, which is an odd item to add in the morning, but Lily couldn't resist. Janet went down to the cafe and grabbed Lily a bowl of jello to eat in the car for when they left the hospital.

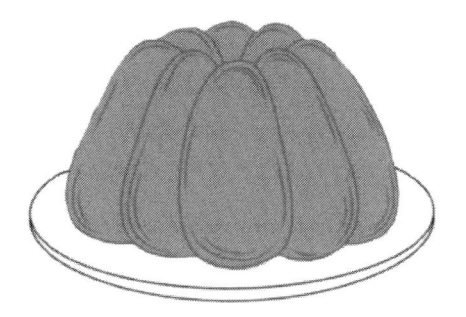

Chapter XX
Released, Ah Home Sweet Home

The afternoon came too fast. The nurse came in and checked Owen and Lily before giving them papers to sign.

"Looks like you can leave, just take those pills and get a lot of rest, Sergeant."

"Will do, thanks, miss."

"You're welcome. Have a good day!"

Owen moaned when he tried getting out of bed, and it took him a minute to get dressed.

"Just tell me if you need help," James hollered.

"Ok."

Lily looked a lot better when she came out of the bathroom with her sweatpants and t-shirt. Janet could tell she was still scared from the events that happened and the disturbing news she had received about her father being murdered. But, she will get her through this tragic time by distracting her mind.

They all left the hospital and jumped in the car. Janet drove James home first, then dropped by Owens place to grab some more of his things. It took Janet a good long minute to find and grab everything for Owen. When she was done, the three rolled up to Lily's father's house. Lily helped carry the bags inside.

"Owen, so you don't have to go upstairs, you can sleep in my father's room."

"Thank you both for letting me stay here."

"No problem, we'll have fun," Lily replied.

The weeks passed quickly, and before they knew it, it was almost July. Lily's bruises were gone and she was back to herself. Owen was stronger and good as new, by the end of June. They binge-watched movies, ordered food, talked all night, and played poker. Now Owen and Lily could finally go on that date, which has been long overdue. James took Janet out some nights and then told Lily and Owen they officially started dating that night.

Janet took Lily upstairs and filled her in on all the juicy details of how he asked her out. Lily loved the kissing part of her story, it got intense and powerful.

When Janet finished Lily had some tea to spill, as well.

"Owen and I watched a movie after you guys left and when I came back from popping popcorn he looked at me differently. He told me I looked beautiful and told me how brave I was. Then he leaned in and kissed me!"

"Oh my god, Lily, that's so cute. He's so hooked on you. Let's go downstairs and ask the boys if they want to go on that double date tomorrow."

"Yeah, Owen and I haven't been out of the house in a few days. But, only if he's feeling alright. I don't want him feeling miserable the whole time."

"Ok, let's go ask!"

Janet and Lily rushed down the stairs with excitement and found the boys eating pizza once again in the kitchen.

"Hey guys, Lily and I were thinking about going to the movies tomorrow. You want to come with us?"

"Yeah, I feel pretty good and it will be fun to get out of the house for a change."

"I have work tomorrow, so can we make it sometime past five?" James asked.

"Yeah. You want to do six-thirty so you have time to get ready?" replied Lily.

"Yep, that's perfect."

"Ok then! We finally get to have our double date. I've been looking forward to it ever since Owen told me."

The four finished the pizza, talking until ten-eleven and decided it was time to call it a night. The next day Janet finished up cleaning with Lily. Lily grabbed tape and a marker and started labeling all the boxes in the living room. Since Lily was a very good organizer, she also stacked the boxes into categories after she labeled them.

After they finished cleaning the house, they took Owen back to his house to unpack and get ready for their night out. Janet and Lily put on their best summer dresses and began getting ready. Owen picked up Lily in his truck and waited for James to pull into the driveway after he got off work. He showed up a few minutes after Owen arrived and told Janet to hop in.

Lily was filled with excitement, she couldn't wait for James and Janet to walk into the theater together as a couple. Owen bought them both two large sodas and one large bowl of popcorn to share. Lily powdered the popcorn and waved over to James and Lily; who were getting their drinks. They all found their seats and watched the movie until the end credits were over. The boys drove Lily and Janet back to the house and both the girls' night ended up with a kiss.

That night Lily had the best sleep she has had in a few weeks. She woke up with a smile on her face. Lily dreamed of the date they went on last night and the time they spent together for the last few weeks. The next day they got dressed and met downstairs for some breakfast. Janet made some more delicious muffins and scarfed them down one by one. Lily left to buy a box of chocolate for Owen's first day back to work. Janet decided to have fun and go shopping until Lily got back from the station.

"I'll be back at the house around noon if you want to do something later," Lily said to Janet as she walked out the door.

"Alright. I have an idea what we can do when you get back," Janet replied.

Lily was glad to see Owen that morning at the station, she could see the excitement in him to be back. He wasn't expecting to see her walk into his office upstairs. Owen stood up and immediately hugged her.

"What are you doing here?"

"I wanted to see how your first day of work was going, and I bought you a little snack."

"Thank you. I'm glad to be back and to make sure those men get what they deserve. Deven will have his trial next week, so I'm happy to be there for that. I think I'm going to eat one of those chocolates now, they look too good."

"Oh, I want one of the chocolate-covered almonds," Lily said to Owen. Owen ripped into the box and ate more than he anticipated. The box of twenty-four was half gone, so he closed it before he was tempted to eat it all. Lily sat in the nice armchair and talked with Owen while he worked and realized it was ten past twelve.

"Owen, I didn't see the time! I told Janet I would meet her back at the house at noon."

"Ok, you want to come over tomorrow night? We can watch a movie and I'll make a romantic dinner?"

"Oh, that sounds charming. What time do you want me over?"

"Is seven a good time?"

"Yeah, that's perfect. I'll see you tomorrow!"

"Ok, love you."

"I love you, too," Lily replied with a smile.

   Lily quickly drove home and saw Janet waiting on the porch with her purse when she pulled in.

"About time," Janet jokingly said to Lily as she shut the car door.

"I know, I was caught up talking to Owen. By the way, tomorrow at seven I'm going over to his house."

"Ok, I'll get James to come over to the house and hang out."

"So, what are we doing?"

"I'm glad you asked. You know how before you were kidnapped the last clue we found was up in the lighthouse?"

"Yeah. I wanted to continue for a while, but we've been distracted. I kind of forgot about the clues."

"I did also for a week or two. I wanted to find it while you guys recovered, but I wanted to wait for you."

"So, you want to go find the next clue? I still have a feeling we're close. I am more than ready. Where does the next clue lead us?"

"The paper says the old mines in the woods. That's near that one house right?" asked Janet.

"Yeah, I believe on the northeast side."

"Well, let's go find that clue," Janet replied excited and ready.

Lily backed out of the driveway and Janet showed her the way to the house; the house they didn't want to see again. Pulling up to the house made her skin crawl. Memories started to pileup. In Lily's head she could see the bedroom she was once locked in. She remembered the drugs pumped into her, the men visiting her every so often. She remembered a pair of eyes that stalked her throughout the night and throughout the day. And she remembered clawing for breath for every second she was beaten by Deven and J.P.! for information she did not know. Lily remembered the hell she went through and with every fiber in her body did not want to be back. Janet came up behind Lily comforting her with a hug. Lily was startled and jumped forward, almost tripping herself.

"I'm sorry, it's just this place. It makes me unsteady. There's an old trail on this side of the woods."

"No, I'm sorry. I just came out of nowhere," Janet replied back.

"It's ok. You know I'm a little jumpy. Let's just go find the mine and get out of these woods."

"Sounds good to me."

Janet and Lily started their journey into the deep woods, walking on the faded path to where she hoped led to the mines. It was never-ending, Janet and Lily felt like they were walking in place. Every tree looked the same and the thick green pine trees overcrowded every neighbor. If the dirt path wasn't visible, they would've been lost within three minutes. Ten minutes of searching went by with still no sign of a mine. The dirt trail was fading into the grass, giving them no more trail to follow.

"How are we going to find the mine now?" Janet yelled at the path.

She turned around and looked at Lily for an answer.

"I don't know. Let's just continue this way and hopefully find it," Lily replied.

"I feel like we've been here forever. It should be here or at least close." When they walked over the next hill they could see the mine entrance about sixty yards away.

"Ok Lily, that looks creepy. Why'd he put it in here? Could've put the clue in the ice cream shop or under another tree, but no, he put it inside a blood-curdling old mine."

"Well, good thing we have flashlights and if anything happens we both have our bracelets on. Let's make sure to stick together," Lily replied.

"Ok, let's do this quickly. I can see cobwebs from here."

Janet and Lily made it down the hill without slipping on the piles of wet leaves below their feet. Lily took out her flashlight and then looked over at Janet, who was suddenly holding a long stick.

"What's that for?" asked Lily.

"I don't want to be covered with spider webs, so I'm going to whip around this stick."

"Good idea, I don't want my face covered either. Hand me the clue and I'll tell you which way to go."

Janet reached into her purse and pulled out the small paper. Lily looked at Janet and turned on the flashlight.

"Ok. You ready, Lily?"

"Yeah, what could go wrong?"

Chapter XXI

Dark tunnels, and a concerning noise

Janet began whipping around her long stick inside the mine, catching every web in their way. The air is heavy with history. Janet turned on the flashlight and its beam pierced through the darkness, revealing the remnants of a forgotten era. The light flickers and dances, casting eerie shadows on the decaying wooden beams and rusty mining equipment.

Janet shined the light on the ground and saw an odd-shaped object. When they walked further in, Janet realized it was just a mining hat. She showed it to Lily and told her she wanted to try it on. Lily warned her about the spiders and other possible bugs that could be inside the hat, and Janet hated bugs.

"Forget it, I don't like bugs."

The girls continued down the dark and dirty tunnel, shining their lights.

"Hey, more tunnels. Which one Lily?"

"Go left."

"Gotcha. I'm hoping no animals are in here. Could you imagine seeing a pair of eyes or hearing a growl in the distance? I'd be scared to death," said Janet.

"There's no need for scary stories. With my luck I would take a wrong turn and get lost here."

The girls slowly made their way down the tunnels and turned right twice. The last turn they made was a dead end, but Lily shined her light up and saw something hanging on the wall.

"What is that?" asked Lily.

"It's a bulletin board and It's really old-looking. Wait, look at this," Janet said to Lily.

   She pointed at a small piece of paper. The only paper without a coat of dust. Lily shines her light on the paper and ripped it off the board.

"Yep, this is it, I see the same star at the bottom!"

"Ok, that was really easy to find. I thought my father would've buried it or hid it in the dirt wall.

"Yeah, right? Let's grab it and get out of here."

"That's exactly what I was thinking," said Janet.

   Lily and Janet made it down the hall and had a few more turns left to go before getting out of the mine. Before they turned the last corner, Lily heard a loud noise. It sounded like a distant growl.

"Did you hear that?" Lily asked Janet with fear in her eyes.

"Yes. How could I not hear that?"

"What should we do Janet? There could be a black bear in here."

"Ok, I went to a camp one summer and they taught me what to do in a situation like this."

"Ok. What do we do?"

"We turn off the flashlight and crouch down."

"Really? Alright."

Lily was terrified and could feel her heart pumping faster and faster. When the lights were off she gripped Janet's jacket and knelt down to the floor.

They sat there for a few seconds and Janet whispered to Lily, "I think it's coming, Lily. It's coming…. Grrrrrrr," Janet screamed out loud.

Lily jumped and almost had a heart attack.

"What the hell Janet, you're going to alert the bear!"

"I hate to tell you this but there is no bear. I was messing with you, it was just my stomach!"

Janet laughed hysterically and Lily gave her a deadly look.

"That was your stomach?"

"Yep, I must be starving. It actually scared me for a second."

Lily wanted to punch Janet so hard, but found herself laughing instead.

"I thought there was a bear or something in here. Don't scare me like that."

"Well, I think we should eat dinner early after hearing that growl."

"You're always thinking about food. But yeah, I'm hungry too. We have that leftover pizza from the other night."

"That's still in the fridge?"

"Yes, I think there's a few supreme slices and one cheese left."

"Good. I want the cheese slice," Janet exclaimed.

"Finally, I see the light!" Lily ran out, excited to see the trees and smell the fresh air.

Janet followed Lily and danced around outside the entrance, singing joyfully.

"We're out, we're out, and we found another clue," she sang.

"You want me to read it?" Lily asked Janet, knowing what her answer would be.

"Yes, read it!"

Lily pulled the paper out of her pocket and began to read.

"Figured out a lot now but

I have more for you, you can

See things that others can't

How you can solve riddles and puzzles is crazy

I'm so proud of you for finding these

Now you will have one more clue after this one.

Get your knife and you'll see four numbers engraved, it will

Show you the combination to the door lock

Have it with you don't forget

And when you open the door look for the picture from the

Car show we went to when you were ten. You got this my

Kind, clever girl, I love you. " *

"We have one more clue after this Lily, but I don't get it though."

"I don't either. He just told us a bunch of scrambled information that didn't add up."

"Let's get out of the woods and figure it out at the house. I don't even want to be in the woods," Lily said, already making her way back to the path.

"Ok, sure. Let's get out of here, I'll drive back."

"Thanks."

   Lily folded the paper and shoved it in her pocket, then turned off her flashlight she forgot was on. The walk felt shorter since they knew how long it would take to get back to the house. The car was hot and uncomfortable and made them both roll down their windows. Lily pulled out the paper and re-read the message written on it over and over. She couldn't figure out where the next clue could be. There was definitely something they were missing.

Janet backed into the driveway and parked in the garage.

Janet raced Lily to the kitchen door and beat her by a second or two.

"I'll warm the pizza. How many pieces do you want, Lily?"

"I'll have three. I'm starving."

Janet warmed the pizza in the oven, while Lily looked at the clue.

"Pizza will be done in five minutes."

"Ok. hey, can you read this? I feel like we're missing a big piece of the puzzle. Usually, I can figure out where the next clue is, but there's nothing here."

"Yeah, I'll look.

Janet read the small piece of paper over and over until the pizza was taken out of the oven.

"Do you have an idea where to go?" Lily asked.

"No, I don't see anything either. But I'm hungry, let's eat."

Lily cut the pizza with the roller and put two pieces on her plate. She wanted to munch on her slice of pizza, but the steam warned her not to dare take a bite just yet.

She looked at the small piece of paper and noticed something she hadn't before. The first letter of every line spelled out 'fishing shack'. Just before Janet was about to sit beside her, Lily jumped out of her chair and yelled "THAT'S IT!"

Janet dropped her plate from being startled. The floor was topped with broken pieces of ceramic and pizza topping scattered around both of their feet.

"GEEZ, Lily. You scared me to death! Look, my pizza is everywhere now."

"We can clean that later. look, I know where to go next!"

"You do?"

"Yeah, he hid it. Look at every first letter of each row. It makes two words."

"Fishing shack?"

"Yep, and I know where it's at, too." Lily continued. "Let's go first thing tomorrow so we're not out too late."

"Yeah, that sounds best. I'm really hungry and I have to go get another slice of pizza because you scared me!"

"I'll clean the mess since I scared you. You should've seen your face when I scared you, it was hilarious."

"Oh, I bet."

Janet grabbed another slice of pizza and didn't worry about how hot it was.

"So, where is the fishing shack exactly?"

"It's on the backside of Clover Lake. My dad built this fishing shed for us to go fishing in the summer. It was the best spot to fish around the whole lake. The combination is engraved on the knife, so it won't take long to get the photo."

"Good. His clues are so clever, I don't think I would've ever noticed that detail," Janet said laughing.

"Yeah, did I tell you he taught high school and middle school English for three years?"

"No, you didn't. That's cool."

"He used to read me poems he wrote in his red journal. I wish I knew where that was. Reading me those every night was one of my favorite memories with him. Then my mom would make all of us hot chocolate with extra marshmallows."

"My mom used to make oatmeal raisin cookies every week and we would have two after dinner. Don't you wish we could go back to those days when we were kids?"

"Yes, all the time."

The pizza was gone and their stomachs were filled. Janet washed the dishes and finished just in time to help carry firewood to the fireplace. Lily and Janet enjoyed the fire for an hour or two, talking and chomping on some popcorn.

Lily slept well that night knowing where the next clue was located. She dreamt of her father and mother making her breakfast and then taking her to the school playground. She waved to her parents going down the frog slide. It was the best one as it was the only slide with bumps and curves. Her parents waved back and clapped when she hit the end. The dream ended with a flash of light and she could hear a voice.

"Wake up, sleepy head!" Janet had opened the drapes and woke Lily up.

   Lily grabbed her blanket and pulled it over her face. Janet jogged over and pulled it off, revealing the light again. She rubbed her eyes with her fists and opened her eyes slowly.

"Janet! I had a good dream going," Lily said in a heartbroken voice.

"Well, we have a lot to do today and it's almost nine."

"Ok, I'll get up."

"I'll see ya downstairs. I warmed up the pancakes we had fixed yesterday."

"Sounds good. I'll be down in a few minutes," replied Lily.

   After the girls finished their stack of chocolate chip pancakes, they grabbed their purses and walked out the kitchen door to the car. Lily drove to the lake and parked in the parking lot.

"It takes about ten minutes to walk to the shack from the parking lot."

"Good thing I wore tennis shoes then," said Janet.

"Yeah, I wasn't thinking. I wore these flimsy sandals."

The lake was calm and serene. The only disturbance was fish jumping out of the lake. Bloop, bloop, bloop.

Lily's feet began to get wet from the dewy grass as they walked further back. She could feel loose blades of grass covering the sides of her feet and in between her toes. They walked over the last hill and could see the shack by the water.

"There it is, Janet. The clue is inside that shack."

"Well, what are we waiting for? Let's go find it."

Lily started running down the hill, but forgot about how wet the grass was. She slipped and fell hard on her butt and started laughing. Lily stood up and tried brushing off the wet grass, but it continued to stick to her pants.

"We don't have all day, Lily," Janet laughed.

"I know, I'm too excited."

"Well, I have the code, so you have to wait for me anyway."

The wood on the shack was rough timber and the window had been dusted over with dirt particles. It was almost camouflaged with overgrown grass hiding the entire bottom of the shack. Stepping stones were pressed into the dirt leading up to the building and the dock.

"You can barely see the stones anymore," Lily said as she looked down.

Lily saw the lock on the door and asked Janet for the pocket knife. She opened the blade and looked at the knife carefully.

"7790," Lily read.

She whispered the numbers to herself over and over until the lock was open.

"Oh, I expected it to be full of junk," Janet said, shocked.

"Because the house was messy when we arrived?"

"Yeah," Janet laughed.

"No, he always kept the fishing shack clean and organized. Now, let's find that picture."

Janet walked to the back and saw some pictures pinned on a small bulletin board.

"Lily, it might be over here."

Lily jumped over to Janet with excitement and looked at the board. They both searched the bulletin board for the picture that was described in the poem, but none of the pictures matched the memory.

"Dang, I thought for sure it would be there. Maybe that's too obvious of a place," Janet said bummed.

"Well, keep looking. It's in here somewhere."

Janet opened the cabinet and checked inside a box that was left at the bottom. No pictures anywhere in sight. Lily grabbed a wooden step stool and checked the higher shelves of the shed, but found nothing. Lily stepped back down, put the step stool back by the door, and looked up at the trim. She saw lines marked on one piece of trim where her father marked her height. She had a different memory for every mark on the trim. Lily remembered every six months her father would measure and mark her growth on the trim. It was always so exciting waiting to see if she had grown taller.

Lily went back to looking and grabbed a fishing tackle box that was on one of the lower shelves. Janet sat on the ground looking through other boxes and glanced back at Lily to see if she made progress. Janet looked up and felt so dumb. There was a picture above the door pinned to the wall.

"Lily, I think I found it."

Lily turned around and then looked up where Janet was pointing. She grabbed the step stool and looked closely at the picture.

"It was there the whole time! Seriously?"

Lily pulled the pin and took the photo outside to get a better look. She remembered that day, looking at the picture. Lily was sitting on her father's shoulder wearing her car shirt and holding a balloon. That day was the day her father bought the car they still have even to this day.

"You were so cute," Janet said behind her.

"Thanks. You know, I wonder." Lily paused then flipped the picture over and saw writing on the back.

"Ah ha, the last clue!"

Chapter XXII

The Last Clue

The girls were filled with exhilaration knowing they were close to finding what her father left for her. Lily immediately started to read the words her father wrote for her.

"I'm so proud of you Lily, you've always loved a challenge. Now the last clue is back at the house where you started. Listen carefully, on our honeymoon we went to this island, find this island and you'll find what I left for you, my girl." *

"Well, looks like we're going back to your fathers house."

"Yep, let's go back home…. But this doesn't make sense."

"What doesn't make sense?" Janet asked, confused.

"Well, my parents never went on a honeymoon," Lily replied back.

"Oh, well, that's just terrific! How are we supposed to figure this one out?"

"I don't know yet. Let's just go back to the car and talk about it."

"Yeah, my shoes are soaked. I really want to take them off."

Lily locked the fishing shack and headed to the car. Lily took a water bottle from the car and poured it onto her wet and grassy feet. All the grass slid down the sides of her feet immediately, and Lily felt a lot better.

"Ok, so lets piece this out a little." Janet said.

Lily pulled the paper out of her pocket and laid it on the arm rest.

"First, we know it's in the house, but we have to figure out what the other part means. How does their non-existing honeymoon tie into finding whatever he hid?" Janet asked.

"I don't know how it ties together, but they went on about six or seven vacations that I know of."

"That's a good start. Try to think of all the trips they went on and I'll write them down," Janet said as she grabbed her small notepad from her purse.

"Ok, I think a few months after I was born they traveled to Tennessee. I remember that because my father said that's when big macs from McDonalds came out."

"Oh, really? Well, that's one."

"Write down Pensacola Beach in Florida, Hawaii, California, Paris, Ireland, and the Bahamas."

"So, that's three islands. One of them is the key to finding what he hid," said Janet.

"Let's go to the house since that is where it is and look around," Lily suggested.

"Yeah. Let's start there."

Lily started the car and when they arrived at the house Lily ran to the hidden room.

"It has to be in here."

"What exactly are we looking for?"

"I'm not sure. Just look for something that involves one of the three islands."

   Janet and Lily started looking around the room. Janet took paintings off the wall, checked every book on the shelves and found nothing. Lily started to wonder if it was in a different part of the house

"Janet, do you want to search the house? Maybe it's not in here."
After she suggested Janet look somewhere else, Lily noticed the globe in the corner of the room.

"WAIT, JANET!" Lily yelled.

She looked at her with a smile.

"I have a crazy idea."

"What's your idea Lily?"

"You see that globe in the corner over there?"

"Yeah, what about it?"

"Well, I was thinking, what if the globe was the hiding place for what he left me. And one of the islands is how to open it. Think about it. The last clue said it was where we started and the island is the key."

"That's a wild thought. I mean the fireplace opening into a room was unexpected. There's only one way to find out!"

Janet ran to the kitchen to grab her notebook she had left on the kitchen table.

"I've got it," Janet gasped.

"Ok, read them off to me."

Janet listed the first one. "Hawaii."

Lily walked around the globe until she found Hawaii. She pushed the island and waited for a few seconds, but nothing happened.

"Ok, try the Bahamas."

Lily pushed all the Bahama Islands, but again nothing happened. There was one left.

"Last one, Ireland," Janet said with her fingers crossed.

   Lily looked up and saw the last island on the globe. She was hesitant at first and almost nervous. They both leaned in and when Lily pressed it the top half of the globe popped off, hitting them both on the forehead. The girls both stepped backwards holding their aching foreheads. Lily had a feeling they were both going to have a headache after that. Lily and Janet leaned towards the open globe. Lily's eyes lit up when she saw what was inside. Her mothers wedding ring, small gold nuggets, a large envelope with the word **Will** written in black ink, and a gold nugget that was a bit bigger than a baseball.

"We did it, Lily! We found it!" Janet said, jumping up and down with Lily.

 Lily cried tears of joy, "Yes, we did. Thank you, father," she whispered to herself.

   It was almost unbelievable. Was this actually happening, she thought? Lily felt like she was in a crazy fairytale, fighting bad guys, dating her dreamy prince charming, getting kidnapped, and finding treasure in the end. Janet and Lily started to take everything out of the globe, and placed it all on the desk. Janet carried the last piece of gold to the desk and observed it. Lily checked inside the globe for anything else and found a small piece of paper that was hidden underneath the large piece of gold. This paper was familiar looking and Lily knew what it was. She put it in her pocket and joined Janet at the desk.

"I'm still in shock, I didn't expect this. Never would I have imagined finding gold."

"Me either. Your father is one of a kind, Lily. One of a kind."

"I was supposed to go out with Owen tonight, but I want to show him this. Maybe he'll know what I can do with this. I mean this has to be the biggest gold nugget in the world."

"Here, Lily," Janet said, handing her the will. Lily grabbed it and looked at the title on the envelope. She paused before opening the envelope, she always dreaded this day. Lily pulled out a sheet of paper and started to read out loud.

" Last Will and Testament Of Josh William Davis

I, Josh William Davis, a resident of Harpswell Maine, on the date 02/22/1991 hereby make, publish and declare this to be my last will and testament, thereby revoking and all previous wills and codicils made by me.

Appointment of Executor/Trustee

I, Josh William Davis, hereby appoint Lillian Grace Davis, daughter, to serve as executor of my will. I wish for anything I or my wife owned to be given to my only daughter Lillian Grace Davis.

Burial

It is my wish to be buried next to my wife Amber Grace Davis in Adam's Grove, Harpswell Maine. All costs and expenses associated with my burial requests shall be paid from the life insurance, if any/or proceeds of my estate.

Signature: __Josh William Davis__ "

A tear rushed down Lily's cheek. She had too many emotions going all at once. Janet pulled Lily in for a hug and comforted her for a minute or two.

"Your father loved you, Lily. He must've known they were coming for him, and wrote this up."

"I never even got the chance to say goodbye to him. I can't believe he left me everything."

Lily wiped her wet face and tucked the will back in the envelope.

"I'm going to get ready. Owen will be off work soon and I'm going to show him all of this. Actually, before I go change I need to tell you something. Since me and Owen have been dating, I was thinking that I would move back up here. I've got Owen and now the house, maybe we could move the business up here."

Janet didn't say anything at first, then smiled.

"I was thinking of asking you if you were going to move up here. I think that's a great idea and I'll move with you. I actually like it here in Harpswell, except for the near death experiences."

"Ok then, should we tell the boys later?"

"Yeah, I'll invite James over and we'll spill the good news."

   Janet and Lily both went upstairs to get ready, then cooked a nice dinner since the plans changed and they were all having dinner together. Janet finished up the mashed potatoes, while Lily got the table ready. The boys showed up not long after and were excited to eat and play games after. Lily rushed to the room behind the fireplace, pulling Owen behind her. His eyes widened, it was the biggest thing of gold he's ever seen. He told her to keep it safe and he would help her figure out a plan on what to do with it.

"I can't believe it. You actually found it."

"Yeah, I'm still in shock. I don't know what to do with it."

"That is the biggest nugget I've ever seen. It's probably museum worthy."

"You know what, Owen? You are brilliant. I'm going to see if any museums want to offer me something for this gold nugget. I will make sure my father's name goes down in history, too."

Lily gave Owen a smile and Owen pulled her close to give her a hug.

"I'm really proud of you."

"Thank you. You know, without you saving my butt multiple times I would've never found this treasure."

"Your welcome, and yeah, you were a pain in the butt."

Lily punched him and laughed. Owen laughed back and looked into Lily's eyes. Their eyes locked with a magnetic attraction, and it gave Lily chills. Lily smiled softly still looking into Owen's eyes and brushed her hand up his chest to his neck and gave him a kiss. He started to stroke her hair and then took full control. He pins her against the wall and continues kissing her intensely. The world around them fades away as they lose themselves in the moment. Their bodies pressed against each other, their hands exploring each others curves, reading them into a new chapter in their relationship.

They finish a few minutes later and decide to join Janet and James for dinner before they start without them. The meal was delicious and disappeared once they sat down. The gravy over the potatoes was perfect and tasted divine with the noodles. Everyone was full and no one could eat another bite. Janet broke the news about moving to Maine and the boys were ecstatic.

"How long until you move in?" James asked.

"Right away, probably. We'll have a struggle getting the business moved over here, but other than that I'll probably take a few weeks," Lily said.

   Janet turned on the radio and pulled James out to dance in the living room. Lily and Owen followed them and danced around until their feet couldn't take it anymore. The night finished with Owen, Lily, James, and Janet passing out on the couch after a few beers. Before Owen and James left in the early morning they grabbed the remaining muffins on the counter. Owen woke Lily up with a kiss on the forehead and walked out the door, waiting for James. Janet wakes up and runs after James in Owen's truck to give him a kiss, as well. The girls both wave goodbye and walk back inside to start their day.

   "What do you want to do today?" asked Janet.

"I was wanting to call the warehouse and try to see when we can get this place going down here. And, I wanted to stop by the cemetery."

"Ok. Go get dressed and I'll meet you down here."

Lily and Janet changed and started making calls to find drivers for shipping their belongings. Janet called the warehouse and explained what was happening to their manager. The morning passed quickly. Lily and Janet didn't even realize they'd been on the phone for three hours.

"Man, I hate making phone calls. People don't understand what I'm saying and it takes ten times longer than it should."
"That's how it always is," Lily replied.

"You want to head over to the cemetery?"

"Yes, I wanted to go there at least before noon"

Before going to the cemetery, Lily stopped and bought two flower bouquets. Lily pulled into the empty parking lot and market in front of the cemetery gate. They walked up the hill and to her parent's graves. She looked down at the stones and read their names.

Lily, do you want me to say a prayer?"

"Lily knelt down and laid the flowers in front of their stones, then looked up at Janet.

"Yes, please," Lily replied.

"Oh Lord, we call upon you in our time of sorrow, that you give us the strength and will to bear our heavy burdens. Keep us forever under your watch, until we can walk again with light hearts and renewed spirits."

"Thanks, Janet."

Lily blew them both a kiss and stood back up.

"I know my dad's happy up there, reunited with my mother."

She told her parents she would visit them every weekend and tell them her stories. Lily shoved her hands in her pockets and felt something rub against her right hand. It was the piece of paper from the globe. She pulled it out and decided to tell Janet.

"Hey, I've waited for the right moment to tell you…. I found something."

"What did you find?"

"At the bottom of the globe was another paper."

She handed it to Janet and Janet's jaw dropped.

"ANOTHER CLUE!"

"Janet, are you ready for another adventure?"

Made in the USA
Columbia, SC
18 June 2024

a80602d5-6108-460c-85bb-a5f6e5469fb0R01